Po... ...the ...urple!
FIC 160

THE A...

W9-AZR-900

DISCARD
The Ag... ...win School
...Middle School Library

THE ULTRA VIOLETS

POWER TO THE PURPLE!

WRITTEN BY

SOPHIE BELL

ILLUSTRATED BY

ETHEN BEAVERS

razOr
bill

An Imprint of Penguin Group (USA) Inc.

razOr bill

A division of Penguin Young Readers Group
Published by the Penguin Group
Penguin Group (USA) Inc., 345 Hudson Street
New York, New York 10014, U.S.A.

USA / Canada / UK / Ireland / Australia / New Zealand / India / South Africa / China
Penguin Books Ltd, Registered Offices: 80 Strand, London WC2R 0RL, England
For more information about the Penguin Group visit penguin.com

Copyright © 2013 Penguin Group (USA) Inc.

All rights reserved. No part of this book may be reproduced, scanned, or distributed
in any printed or electronic form without permission. Please do not participate in or
encourage piracy of copyrighted materials in violation of the author's rights. Purchase only
authorized editions.

Published simultaneously in Canada

Library of Congress Cataloging-in-Publication Data is available

ISBN: 978-1-59514-647-2

Printed in the United States of America

1 3 5 7 9 10 8 6 4 2

This is a work of fiction. Names, characters, places, and incidents either are the product of
the author's imagination or are used fictitiously, and any resemblance to actual persons,
living or dead, businesses, companies, events, or locales is entirely coincidental.

For Diamond Eila

Starting with a Bang
{Yes, That's Right, We're Beginning with Chapter 2}

WIELDING HER HANDS LIKE TWO LASER LIGHT SABERS, purple ringlets whipping behind her as she turned, Iris took aim and—*zzvonk! zzvomp!*—sliced blistering twin beams of rainbows through the air. The multicolored blades slashed within a hairsbreadth of Opaline's body, and she staggered back into the lockers. "Owie!" she screeched, feeling the heat. Her arms flailed at her sides, spastic with her own high voltage. But quickly she regained control and returned fire, flicking off lightning bolts between her fingers as if they were arrows in a bow. Iris took one hit to the shoulder— "Ungh!"—another to the hip—"Oof!"—the crackling electric daggers stabbing through the flimsy fabric of her dress. "That was brand-new!" she cried, furious, and fanned out a shield of pure ultraviolet rays to block the next lightning spear. It exploded into the invisible barrier, bursting into a thousand electric embers. And the duel flared on, blazing beams versus lightning bolts, searing sunshine versus heavy

1

storm clouds. Out of the corner of her eye, Iris could see Scarlet, her ponytail glowing aubergine. She had the lizard girl by the tail and was swinging her over her head so fast that it created a vortex right there in the hallway. The wind blew Iris's hair back. And Opal's cloud away. The strange two-faced cheerleader on the sidelines kept rah-rah-ing. Then Cheri's voice carried above the fray.

"Stop it, you guys!" she called. "Dingelmon's coming!"

At the sound of the principal's name, Opaline lost her focus for just a second. That was all Iris needed. She pinned Opal against the lockers, pressing her hot forearm across Opal's shoulders like the bar that bolts you in on an amusement park ride. The two girls glared eye-to-eye—Opal's brown orbs streaked with milky swirls, Iris's blues shining a whiter shade of pale.

"Opaline," she panted, recoiling once more at the strange, gross smell wafting from her frenemesis. "Keep your hands off the skunk."

"Whatever." Opal tried to laugh, but the pressure from Iris's arm made it hard for her to breathe. "Soon I'll have the whole school at my command. So you can keep your stinky little mascot."

The bell *braaaanged* and the girls broke apart. Opal shrugged off Iris's arm, electric volts still fizzing around her shoulders. Shaking, she swung her hand in a wide circle, snapping her fingers twice: once above, once below. "Fall in, O+2!" she ordered. Shoved forward by Scarlet, the lizard girl limped alongside her. The beatnik cheerleader brought up the rear, her orphan pompom rustling like a bad breeze.

"Have a super-sparkly day!" Scarlet shouted after them.

With Opaline and her hangers-on shuffling away, Cheri stepped back into the middle of the hallway, clutching Darth close in her tote bag. Scarlet straightened out the tiers of her tutu. Iris examined the holes in her dress.

"Well, that's one way to start the school week," Scarlet muttered.

"Lizards give me the creeps," Cheri said, tapping out a quick post to all her Smashface friends to defend Iris and deny the juice rumor.

"Lizards I can deal with," Scarlet huffed. "But a two-faced cheerleader? Now *that's* creepy!"

"What the swell was that smell?" Iris wondered, unwrapping a fresh lollipop. "And why did Opaline want Darth?"

Before they could discuss it any further, the booming bass voice of their principal snapped them to attention.

"Didn't you girls hear the bell?" he said.

"Sorry, Mr. Dingelmon!" the three Ultra Violets chorused sweetly. Then they dashed off to class.

O No She Didn't
{Fifteen Minutes Before the Bang}

WAIT, WHAT JUST HAPPENED? HOW DID WE GET HERE?
And where is here, anyway?

A long time ago, in a galaxy far, far away?

Not.

The morning after the night before the weekend after the school trip when three besties officially became secret superheroes and the fourth went all evil on them?

Oh swell yes.

And so it begins. Or rather continues. This being the start of the *second* saga of the purple-empowered Ultra Violets and the villainy Opaline, aka the girl that got away. Here being a sort of alternate universe, in the twinkling city of Sync, at an oddly egg-shaped school called Chronic Prep. Now being fifteen minutes before the rainbow laser beam blasts.

As Iris Tyler rushed to join the throng of students streaming into the school that morning, her long, lilacalicious ringlets bounced all the way down her back. And if you had special infra-violet goggles, you might also spy a faint purple aura pulsating all around her, as pale as her periwinkle eyes. Iris's classmates knew about the purple hair—since it was totes obvious—but not about the aura. Or about Iris's ability to mind-paint things whatever color she wanted. Or shoot blazing ultraviolet rays from her eyes. Or beam out a rainbow with just a wave of her hand.

The only people who knew about that stuff were her girls, Cheri and Scarlet.

And also their bestie gone rouge, er, rogue, Opaline Trudeau.

And ALSO their erstwhile (*that means "used-to-be"*) babysitter, Candace Coddington—more on her later.

But that's it!

Standing outside the school's revolving doors, Cheri Henderson snuck a grape to a grapeful Darth Odor, the sweet little violet-striped skunk hidden in her bag. Then, from beneath the veil of her berry-red hair, she freshened up her bubblegum lip gloss.

"Careful!" Scarlet Louise Jones gave her friend a playful poke in the ribs. Cher answered with a yelp as her hand slipped.

"Scar!" she exclaimed with a stamp of her platform roller skates. A dab of glittery pink gloss now decorated the tip of her nose.

Scarlet giggled at the sight and sprang away, her black ponytail popping up like an exclamation point, before Cher could poke her back.

She kidz bcuz she luvs, Darth thought, sticking his nose out of Cheri's bag.

Well, the way Scarlet spells it, love is a four-letter word! Cheri thought back, rubbing the stray gloss from her nose. True, love was a four-letter word no matter who spelled it. But ever since Cher had developed supersonic math skills, she couldn't help counting everything in her head. And ever since she'd developed animal telepathy, she liked to think things over with Darth.

Scarlet glid (*that's how we spell it*) back toward Cheri just as Iris joined the two girls at the entrance.

"Hey," Iris said with a smile.

"Hi, Iris!" Cheri said back, while Scarlet greeted her with a graceful *demi-plié*.

Iris took in Scarlet's outfit: battered kicks, black leggings, rock-n-roll T-shirt, and . . . "The tutu is killer, Scar," Iris exclaimed, her eyes widening. "Totally you."

"Whatever that means." Scarlet shrugged, slightly embarrassed, then continued her twirling within one Plexiglas wedge of the revolving door. Cheri rolled into the school building behind her. Iris followed. Getting slimed four years ago with crazy-goo had given Iris her purple hair and color-prism powers. It had gifted Cheri with her beautiful brains.

Scarlet got dancing.

Uh-huh. Her superpower was dancing.

And she was still trying to deal.

She'd scanned the comic-book collections of all three of her older brothers, and as far as she could find out, dancing was NOT a traditional superpower. So at first Scarlet had been kind of irked and kind of freaked to find herself spontaneously pirouetting. But her cancan kicks *had* come in handy on more than one strange occasion already. And all of a sudden she found satin ballet slippers *terribly* pretty—though, being more tomboy than girly-girl, Scarlet didn't go around announcing that through a bullhorn. Yet here she was, wearing a tutu to school. It was all a bit confusing. She—repeat—was still trying to deal!

As the three girls (plus secret skunk) made their way down the hall and toward their homeroom, Iris began to feel self-conscious. The Jensen sisters skittered by, their high-pitched whispers whistling through the gaps in their twin buck teeth. Brad Hochoquatro elbowed Ian Rundgren when he saw her, and the two boys broke out in guffaws. Was Iris just imagining things, or was everyone talking about her? After four years away, she'd been back in Sync City and at Chronic Prep for some time now, purple hair and all. She thought she was past that awkward "new girl" phase. But . . . maybe not? She could feel the eyes of other students on her, and their harsh laughter scratched at her ears. Her cheeks began to burn, and she tried to hide her red face behind her violet ringlets as she fumbled with her locker.

Down the hall, Cheri was just placing a few books in her locker when Julie Nichols stopped by.

"Cheri!" she said breathlessly. "Did you hear?"

Ooh, gossip! Cheri thought. Just what she needed to juice up her morning. "No, what?" she gushed. "Tell me!"

"Check your Smashface page," Julie called back as she continued toward their classroom. "Or text me and I'll send you a link!"

Cheri took out her smartphone just as Scar and Iris joined her. They gathered around while Cheri pulled up her Smashface page, Scarlet simply curious, Iris filled with dread.

Cheri scrolled down her screen, then frowned. "Oh, it's actually nothing," she said, trying to sound nonchalant as she hurried to put her phone away again.

"Wait, what does it say?" Scarlet demanded, shooting up *en pointe* in her sneakers and taking out her own phone. Iris asked softly, "C'mon, Cher. It's something about me, isn't it?"

Cheri's green eyes were bright. "It's just a stupid Smashface post," she said, dismissing it with a wave of her sparkly silver manicure. "Everybody knows you can't believe half of what you read there."

"You dye your hair with prune juice?!" Scarlet blurted out, finding the post, too. Her voice boomeranged around the corridor, and the other kids all turned to stare at the trio. "That's ridic!" Scarlet said more quietly, coming back down to first position. "And—"

"And apparently my hair's 'not the only thing that's purple,'" Iris finished for her, reading the post off Cheri's phone. Cheri bit her lower lip. "Nice," Iris added.

"Ignore it!" Cheri tried to reassure her. "They're just jealous!"

"And it's not like we can tell everyone your hair is purple because, oh, BTdubs, your DNA got altered in a Heliotropium accident in the FLab four years ago!" Scarlet muttered, glancing around to make sure no one else could hear them.

"I know," Iris agreed with a sigh, distressed all the same. "But who started this rumor, anyway? Who's supposedly so 'jealous'?"

The three girls stared at the post, Scarlet on her own phone, Iris and Cheri on Cheri's. At the bottom, they noticed what looked like a logo: a white circle outlined in black, with an acid-yellow lightning bolt cutting across it.

"*O*," Iris said, her lips forming the shape of the letter.

"*O* no," Cheri whispered.

"*O* sugarsticks," Scarlet practically spat.

"*O* na na, what's my name?" a singsong voice echoed off the lockers.

The Ultra Violets looked up from the phone screens to see a girl standing across from them in the shadowy hallway. A starched Peter Pan collar stuck out above the neckline of her yellow velour tracksuit. A quilted black lightning bolt blazed across her chest. And microscopic volts of electricity sparked from her shoulders.

"Opaline!" Iris growled in spite of herself, the white-violet aura intensifying and her purple corkscrews vibrating with currents of their own.

An anxious energy filled the corridor. Even though Chronic Prep was carefully climate-controlled, the temperature inside the school felt hot and humid all of a sudden. Sensing the rising stress levels, all the other students scooted off to their homerooms, casting nervous glances at the clutch of girls who remained. Iris stepped into the center of the hallway; Cheri and Scarlet lined up behind her. Cher planted her platforms firmly on the floor. Scar clenched her hands into fists at her sides and drew one foot up in a delicate *coupé* arc beneath her knee.

Opal sauntered across the hall to meet them, flanked by two other girls. At first the UVs couldn't remember ever having seen them before. But then they recognized trendoid Karyn Karson with her lank spaghetti-blond strands and a slithery lizard tail poking out from the waistband of her skinny jeans. The second girl seemed to be suffering from acute, uncute, split personality disorder. Head to toe, one half of her was all gloom and goth, the other all perky and pep squad. Like a cheerleader crossed with a Twihard. Which was a way less adorable combo than a pug-beagle puggle. (Cheri would know: She volunteered at an animal shelter.)

"Mutants!" Scarlet whispered.

Iris gave a subtle nod, her ringlets barely bobbing behind her.

Cheri just thought, *Ew.*

Dubble ew! Darth thought back, peeking out of the tote bag at the two-faced girl.

You see (*if you've already read the first book, you can skip this paragraph*), the Ultra Violets were not the only weirdness happening in Sync City, as the girls had recently discovered. It was strange enough that they had grown superpowers four years after getting doused with triple-top-secret Heliotropium goo in the Fascination Laboratory, or FLab, where their doctor-moms all worked. But just across the river, in an abandoned mall, at a company called BeauTek, a rival lab, the Vi-Shush, seemed to be . . . maybe . . . Cheri was 99.9 percent certain . . . well, that the Vi-Shush was manufacturing mutants.

Mutants!

Monster ew! Darth added, hearing Cher's mind.

The girls weren't sure exactly what was up at BeauTek. But you didn't have to be a superbrain like Cheri to know that a mutant factory mall was definitely not a positive development. The Ultra Violets had vowed that, with the help of their erstwhile (*that means "once-upon-a-time"*) babysitter Candace, they'd do everything in their power to protect the citizens of Sync City from these hideous creatures.

Even if those citizens were completely clueless about the fact that their lives now depended on three middle-school girls.

But back to the pre-bang hallway. Where Opaline Trudeau, the girl who had gone rouge-slash-rogue, was standing in her Peter Pan–collared tracksuit, staring down her ex-bestie Iris Tyler.

"Opal," Iris said, trying to smile. Not long ago at all, they'd promised to be BFFs. As much as Opal had upset her since then, Iris was still determined to get her back on Team Ultra Violet. "I know we have, um, issues, but did you really have to go and post lies about me to the whole school?"

Opal smirked in response. "Would you prefer I post the truth?" she taunted, batting her lashes. Tiny white storm clouds streamed across her brown eyes. "About you and your 'Ultra Violets'? Like anyone would believe it."

"No, of course not!" Iris said. She could feel her fingertips throbbing with heat, and she took a deep breath to keep from solar-flaring. "But with all the freakiness on parade from the Mall of No Returns"—Iris's gaze shot from lizardlike Karyn to Goth Cheerleader before landing on Opal again—"I thought you might want to reconsider my . . . offer."

"Ha!" Opal's short, sharp laugh sounded more like a hacking cough. She leaned forward, so close to Iris that their foreheads were almost touching, and said in a voice too low for her new friends to hear. "You mean to join the Ultra Violets? And save Sync City from a mutant invasion?"

Iris shoved her hands into her pockets, where they glowed through the gauzy cotton of her brand-new dress. Her eyes began to tear, and she scrunched up her nose: Something smelled so wrong—Opal's shampoo? But that couldn't be it: The stench was faint but foul, like sweat socks blended with brussels sprouts. What girl would ever wash her hair with that? "Yeah," Iris said, trying not to breathe in any more of the funk, "that offer."

"Hmm." Opal pretended to think about it, twirling a finger around a strand of her brown hair in mocking imitation of Iris. Then she snarked, "OMV, thanks!" and tilted her head from shoulder to shoulder. Behind her, K-Lizard and Goth Cheerleader did the same, snapping their hair back and forth robotically. "But no thanks," Opal continued, dropping her voice so it rumbled like thunder. "We are never ever ever getting back together, UVs. Because guess what? *I'm* the one bringing that mutant invasion. And I'm going to make all the kids in our class serve *me*. *And* I've already got some superbesties of my own."

"You do?" Scarlet furrowed her brow. "Where?" She sprang straight up in a *grand changement* jump, scanning the hallway for more superheroes. Maybe they were invisible. Maybe that's why she couldn't see them.

"Duh, Scarlet." Opal rolled her eyes, then jerked her head back toward her hair-tossing posse. "You already know Karyn—"

Karyn curled her thin lips into a smile, a forked tongue flicking out between her fangs.

"—and this is BellaBritney." Opal hitched her thumb at the dour cheerleader.

"Bella—" Scarlet began.

"—Britney?" Cheri completed.

"Ugh," the gothy Bella side mumbled through a half-mouth of black lipstick at the exact same moment the hyper Britney side cheered, "Yay!" with a wave of her single pompom.

18

It was jarring, to say the least. Darth let out a disturbed squeak.

"Those two?" Cheri said, astonished. (She wasn't quite sure if BellaBritney counted as one whole or two halves or what.) "But Opal, sweetie, they're not superheroes at all! They're, like, the complete opposite, because they're—"

"O+2!" Opal boomed, drowning out the *M* word before Cheri could even utter it.

The hallway shook, and if any teachers had bothered to look out from their classrooms they might have noticed a black storm cloud hovering just below the ceiling. "Opaline plus two," she said, directly at Iris. "O+2. Dioxide. Maybe you're familiar with it? It's a key ingredient in sunscreen." Opal snickered. "It blocks UV rays."

"*In-ter-ception!*" BellaBritney half-cheered again, as if she were at a football game.

The beams from Iris's fists intensified, and as she stared back at Opal, her pale blue eyes began to glow, too. "I don't know, Opes," she said, her voice in cool contrast to all the heat she was radiating, "The sun can be pretty strong . . ."

Above the girls, the gathering storm cloud growled.

From the bottom of the tote bag, Darth nudged up a pink polka-dot umbrella. Cheri opened it as a preventive measure. "Oh, Opal," she pleaded, pinching her nose at the putrid stench she'd just detected drifting out from behind her ears. "I know you're still steamed about our little misunderstanding over"—Cheri cleared her throat and tried to rush past the boy's name—"Albert, but please don't make it rain in here, okay?" she asked. "It took me *forever* to blow out my hair this morning."

At the mention of Albert Feinstein, Opal flinched. The four girls had promised to be BFFs, had even sealed it with a candle-wax pinkie swear. But then Opal caught Cheri kissing her crush . . .

Opal scoffed. Clearly, "forever" didn't last much longer than a blowout.

"You know what, Cher?" she said, stepping closer. "I don't even want Albert anymore. I just want what's mine. What you took from the Vi-Shush!" With a swing of her hand and a snap of her fingers, Opal commanded, "Karyn!"

K-Liz snaked out her reptilian tail, coiling it around the handle of Cheri's tote bag.

"Give me back that skunk!" Opal shouted.

"OMV, what?! Never!" Cheri cried, bashing at K-Liz's tail with her polka-dot umbrella.

The thunder boomed. Iris whipped her hands out of her pockets, already powered up. Scarlet pirouetted into a kickbox, knocking K-Liz off her feet.

And *that* was how the bang began.

(*Go back to the first page just in case you've forgotten!*)

Why O Why?

ARE M&M'S AND SKITTLES FIRST COUSINS? HOW MANY licks *does* it take to get to the center of a Tootsie Pop? Is some old lady somewhere still sucking on the original Everlasting Gobstopper? Does Chocolate Mountain melt over summer vacation in Candy Land? And why is Mars the only planet to get its own candy bar? Wouldn't Jupiter want one, too?

These are the questions that have tormented philosophical trick-or-treaters since the dawn of time. And now, for the Ultra Violets, a new imponderable was added to that list:

Why did Opaline Trudeau, once as sweet as a Pixy Stix, turn into such a Sour Patch Kid?

"Every time I try to explain about Albert," Cheri bemoaned, "she just cuts me off with a sudden rain shower!" From beneath the frilly canopy of the schoolyard fluffula tree, Cheri glanced up at the midday sky. There wasn't a cloud in sight.

"Well," Scarlet said, hopping little balletic *temps levé* jumps in place, "you really shouldn't have kissed him."

"I didn't kiss him!" Cheri cried, her cheeks blazing in protest. "He kissed me!" Right there, as a matter of fact, beneath that very fluffula tree.

"Tomayto, tomahto!" Scarlet answered in *arabesque*, struggling to keep a straight face. Deep down she knew that Cheri really hadn't meant for Albert Feinstein to kiss her— on the contrary, Cher had been trying ultra hard to give the boy a stealth makeover for Opaline! But since Albert *had* kissed Cher, no way was Scarlet going to miss out on all the many opportunities to tease her about it.

"Maybe, from Opal's point of view," Iris mused, examining the ends of one violet tendril, "who kissed whom might be splitting hairs."

"Alas!" Cheri sighed, blowing a strand of her own berry-red waves out of her eyes, raising an arm to her forehead, and falling back against the trunk of the legendary tree with all the theatricality of an actress. "I can only say sorry so many times! Twenty-three, at last count!"

From a branch above her, Darth practiced his dramatic swoon, too.

"I hear you, Cher," Iris said from her spot on the squat Plexiglas wall that bordered the yard. "I think the Albert thing was just . . ."

" . . . Opal's breaking point," Scarlet finished, balancing *en pointe* herself.

"Right," Iris agreed. She began to ultra-doodle, painting imaginary blue butterflies in the air with her pinkie finger. "We just have to remember, we have to *believe*, that the old Opaline, the real Opaline, is still somewhere behind those clouded eyes." Iris said it as a reminder to herself as much as to her friends. Since Opal had gone evil, she'd electroshocked Iris twice, teamed up with mutants, and shattered Iris's lollipop peace offering after the showdown in the Vi-Shush.

Then there was the prune juice rumor just that very morning.

And the threat against the entire student body of Chronic Prep?

Oh, and she wanted to steal Darth!

OMV.

"The way she's behaving is not totally under her control," Iris continued, trying to keep her thoughts from going all sour-pruney, too. "She had a bad reaction to the Helio-goo."

"On a *deoxyribonucleic* level!" Scarlet intoned, imitating Candace's serious scientist voice.

When they'd last met with Candace, their erstwhile (*ahem*) babysitter, in the rock-crystal Fascination Laboratory on the forty-second floor of the Highly Questionable Tower, the Ultra Violets had pledged to bring Opal back from the dark side. Because she really was one of them. Even if these days she kept acting like a superbrat.

The Ultra Violets fell silent for a moment, each considering the trouble with Opal and her scary talk of taking over the school. Then Cheri looked from Scarlet to Iris. She hesitated a moment more, and Darth scampered down from the tree branch to her shoulder to give her some moral support. Cheri ran her sparkling silver fingernails through the little skunk's purple-striped tail as she said, "I still believe in the inner Opal, too. But . . ."

Iris and Scarlet waited, Iris's doodling pinkie paused in midair, Scarlet's arms outstretched in second position.

"But the *probability* is," Cheri stated, "that the Opal drama is going to get worse. Much worse. Before it gets better. If it ever gets better."

Iris's blue eyes flashed with alarm. "What do you mean, Cher?"

"And how do you know?" Scarlet demanded, arching one arm above her head in third position.

Cheri glanced at Darth.

U gotz to tel dem, he said, nodding his stripy skunk head.

"I sort of . . ." She began over. "It's hard to explain, but . . ."

Iris leaned forward, listening intently, as Scarlet dropped her other arm to her side in fourth position.

"My brain computated the odds," Cheri said, blushing again. Her mom and dad, as well as the girls' doofy rapping math teacher, Mr. Grates, would disagree if only they knew, but Cheri still thought her arithmeticulous superpowers were neither the coolest nor the funnest. Plus, they had also added to the problems with Albert! Which, minus, had subtracted one friend! And—

"Earth to Cheri," Scarlet prompted, both arms now raised in fifth position. "We're waiting!"

"Okay," Cheri said, cradling Darth in her arms. She raised her eyebrows at the girls, almost as if she were apologizing for what she was about to say. And then she live-streamed the data:

"Calculating the estimated number of mutants in Sync City, their allegiance to Opaline, and the degree of importance she must derive from bossing them around"— as Cheri spoke, an electric green pattern of numbers and symbols scrolled down her eyes, just like programs on a computer monitor, and her hair suddenly seemed to shine with a magenta tint—"the dominant outcome for the ten most likely scenarios is that Opal will lead, um, what did she call it again?"

"O+2," Iris said somberly.

"Yes. She'd rather be alpha-girl over a bunch of mutants than work with us. So there's no O in team."

"But how can you possibly calculate something like that?" Scarlet spluttered. Having rotated through the basic arm positions in ballet, she'd saddled up and started to ride a pretend pony, Gangnam-style. "How can you calculate how Opal *feels*?"

"EQ," Cheri said, her eyes clear green and her hair just auburn again. "It's like IQ, but for emotions. No matter how I adjust the EQ percentages in the equations, the probability comes out the same." She sighed, hugging Darth close for comfort. "Sorry, guys."

"But surely, as brilliant as your superbrain may be, Cher, we can't predict everything!" Iris said, her voice strained with worry. How could they possibly win Opal back if the math already told them the odds would never be in their favor?

"True," Cheri allowed, because people were the most difficult problems to solve, even with the most advanced computer programs. "There could be a black swan."

"A black swan?!" Scarlet repeated, straightening up. That very *pas de deux* from *Swan Lake* was the first ballet she'd ever superdanced, at home in her own basement. And with her licorice-dark ponytail and dove-gray eyes, she thought she quite looked the part.

A black swan?! Darth exclaimed. Having ebony fur himself, he found the idea of a big black-feathered bird intriguing.

"Not an actual black swan," Cheri said, stroking Darth on his nose. "Or a black swan ballerina," she added to Scarlet. "A black swan is the name for this, like, idea where something totally strange happens. Something you didn't count on happening. Something that you never even knew *could* happen. Until it does. And then it changes everything."

Crestfallen, Scarlet squatted back down again and resumed her Gangnam dancing with vigor. "Oh," she said. "So I guess that means I can't dance Opal back to being good."

"Sorry, Scar," Cheri said, frustrated afresh by her brainy superpowers. "They call it that because nobody thought there could be such a thing as a black swan, until they saw one and realized there was."

"Like us!" Iris said thoughtfully. "Whoever would have imagined we'd become purple-powered superheroes till we did?"

"I can definitely be the black swan," Scarlet countered, still stuck on the ballet. "I can do that *adagio* in my sleep."

"Whoa!" From her perch on the Plexiglas wall, Iris began to quake. "Hey, Scar, take it easy!"

Scarlet had been so obsessed with *Swan Lake*, she hadn't quite realized just how hard she'd been stomping the yard. Every step she took sent vibrations across the ground. The Plexiglas wall wobbled, nearly uprooted from its posts, while feathery crimson leaves floated down from the shaken fluffula tree.

"Eep!" Scarlet squeaked, dropping to the grass and wrapping her arms around her knees to keep them still. "I've been noticing," she confessed, her freckles like teeny poppy seeds above the pouf of her red tutu skirt, "that I might not totally know my own strength. Er, yet."

"I kn-kn-kn-know!" Iris's voice wavered along with the Jell-O-ing wall. "I s-s-saw the w-w-way you th-threw around K-Karyn!"

"The other day I dropped my phone," Scarlet said, her fingers still drumming a techno beat across her kneecaps. "And I lifted up the couch with one hand to get it."

"The whole couch?" Cheri was astonished. "Did anyone see?"

"No, luckily," Scarlet said. "But I've got to be careful, because we've got to keep our powers secret! Imagine what new chores my mom might make me do if she knew!" Scarlet did *not* want to get stuck picking up her three brothers' grungy beds while her dad vacuumed beneath them on Saturday mornings.

"Hey!" Iris realized, jumping down from the wall to sit by Scarlet. "Maybe that's the black swan idea you meant, Cher! Maybe, if all our powers are still developing, then Opal's could still turn good!"

"Mmmaybe . . ." Cheri said, spreading out her tote bag like a picnic blanket to sit on. Though she wasn't so sure. And by that logic, wouldn't it also mean that any of them could still turn bad? What a terrible thought! Cheri shook her head to knock it out of her stupid supermind! Darth, the only one who'd heard it, swished his purple-striped tail right along with her.

Scarlet wondered if music was playing that only Cheri and her skunk could hear. "Um, Cher?" she asked, staring at the shimmying auburn fringe. "Are you okay?"

Cheri realized what she was doing. "Aftershock?" she offered from behind a curtain of hair, because she didn't want the other UVs to know what had really set her off. She tried to get their conversation back on track and her hair back in place. "Why, Iris?" she said, borrowing her brush. "Are your powers still changing, too?"

Iris beamed a big smile, and it was as if the sun shone

right out of her eyes. "Check this out," she whispered. With a deep breath, she closed her eyes and flung herself back against the grass. As Scarlet and Cheri watched, she seemed to vanish. Her arms, her face and her clothes all picked up the pattern of the lawn. All that remained were hints of her purple ringlets. When she blinked her periwinkle eyes open again, the blue stood out like two bright bird eggs in the green blades.

"Oh. My. Crazy. Violet," Cheri gasped. "Just like a chameleon!"

"Cool!" Scarlet said, tumbling to her feet again.

"Camouflage." Iris sat up, turning back to all her normal colors. "Maybe being able to blend in will come in handy."

"Yeah!" Scarlet agreed, rocking a little hip-hop on the grass. In the distance, she could see the other kids starting to line up as recess came to an end. "To spy on mutants!"

"Or on Opaline?"

Cheri was the one who said it. But it was what all three of them were thinking.

Geek Love

TO THE LIST OF QUESTIONS THAT TORMENT PHILO-
sophical types, let's add another. A question that's more
Valentine's Day than Halloween. A question you might see
stamped on a jumbo pastel candy heart:

Why do fools fall in love?

A simple answer might be that almost *everybody* falls in
love sooner or later, and some of those everybodies, sorry
to say, are fools. But other of those everybodies are not
fools at all. They're brilliant. They're geniuses. They're even
mathlete captains.

Thus brings us to the curious case of Albert Feinstein.

Remember what Albert looks like? No? Good, because he
doesn't look like that anymore. He looks a lot better, merci
to Cheri and her stealth makeover that led to the seismic
unfortunate fluffula tree kiss-off. In fact, Albert was now
one of the most stylin' boys in the sixth grade. His sandy-
blond crew cut had grown into a touchably tousled mop,

his braces glinted with a grill of gold, and he had finally mastered the art of walking in unlaced high-tops. Lots of girls liked him now—not Cheri, and not the UVs, not in *that way*. But other girls.

Behind his fly aviator frames, though, Albert only had eyes for Opaline Trudeau.

Wait! you're thinking. *Isn't this the same boy who crushed on Cheri while Opal was crushing on him?* Yes, that's the correct recap! A+! But like a dollar in a vending machine, change happens. After Cheri not-so-gently declined Albert's advances, he decided that such a glamazon might not be the girl for him after all. For while Albert was kind of a rock god on the outside, on the inside he was still a math geek.

And his geek heart now beat for the mysterious Opaline Trudeau.

Opaline didn't blind Albert's glasses with shiny lip gloss and sparkly nail polish and sequined headbands like Cheri Henderson did. Quite the opposite. With her perfectly linear part and her chocolate brown hair pinned back at precisely equidistant points in simple barrettes, with her plain white shirt buttoned all the way up to its sweet Peter Pan collar, Opal reminded Albert of an eleven-year-old version of his very first librarian. So prim and proper, it was driving Albert crazy. In a good way. In *that way*.

Opaline Trudeau was like the trickiest brainteaser ever, and Albert Feinstein was dying to solve it.

His mathlete mind was whirring in overdrive with all these nonnumerical thoughts as he took his seat in math class after recess. He watched, enraptured, when Opal entered the room and glid (*our spelling!*) to her alphabetically dictated desk way at the back (and just in front of that artsy Iris Tyler with her purple curls). Albert caught Opal's eye, and one quizzical look from her caramel brown orbs sent his lenses into a fog. As Mr. Grates began his rhyming lecture about "relative coordinates" at the front of the class, Albert decided an old-school move would be most romantic (at least that's what his mom always told him). Sure, he could have tried texting Opal, or besmashing her on Smashface, or sending her a direct tweek.

But no. He was going old-school!

He took his best blue pen from the secret pocket protector he still wore on the inside of his T-shirt. While Mr. Grates got jiggy with integers, Albert tugged a blank page from his notebook as quietly as he could. He folded the sheet. Used his protractor to map an expertly symmetrical shape. And then traced the outline with the ballpoint until the border was thin enough to tear.

It was a heart-shaped note.

On it, he wrote:

Me + U = Saturday Chess?

It was the most elementary equation he could think of.

Then he added a circle. Two decimal points. And a sideways parenthesis:

☺

Applying the principles of aerodynamics, Albert folded his paper heart into a paper plane. With Mr. Grates out of sight—on the floor of the classroom doing the caterpillar—Albert set his note in flight. For a second he feared it would be intercepted by that horn-headed dolt Duncan Murdoch. But it landed directly on Opaline's desk.

Albert pivoted back around in his seat, pretending to pay attention. And buzzing with anticipation!

Behind Opal, Iris was, naturally, curious about the note. But after the prune juice rumor and their morning duel, she chose to keep a low profile. Even before "the change," Opal could be sensitive about boy-girl stuff. And when it came to Albert Feinstein, there wasn't just math; there was *history*. So Iris didn't say a word. She tried to be subtle as she peered over Opal's shoulder. But Opal bowed her head, her straight brown hair swinging down like a curtain closing on her desktop. Iris couldn't see a thing.

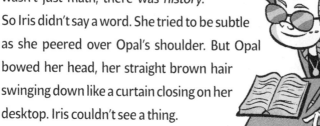

Opaline was not in a happy place. She hadn't been, really, ever since all this drama started with the Ultra Violets. She couldn't understand why. She had superpowers now, just like Iris, Scarlet, and Cheri. With a snap of her fingers and a spark of electricity, she could shock mutants like K-Liz and BellaBritney into obeying her every command. And she was wearing the most stunning—no, seriously, *stunning*—new BeauTek scent. Yet a crabby camper was she.

So when Opal saw Albert's sweet, sketched smiley on his ragged valentine, for a moment her heart lifted and, behind the shadow of her hair, she smiled, too. She remembered the sleepover at Scarlet's house, where she'd confessed her crush on the mathlete captain. She imagined what it might be like to hang out with Albert, playing chess or just sudoku, maybe sharing a peach soda. For that fleeting instant, his paper heart open on her desk, its creases carefully smoothed out beneath her fingertips, it all seemed possible again.

But then she looked up. At Albert's trendy new haircut and T-shirt, at his thick hip-hop b-ball sneakers—as if he were an actual athlete, not just a mathematical one. It all seemed a bit fake. Albert may have been a geek before, but Opal had liked him just the way he was: with his high-waisted khakis, his proud pocket protector, and his shirt buttoned all the way to the top, just like hers.

Albert wasn't showing any signs of mutantism. But, her heart sinking back down to the pit of her stomach, Opal wondered if he might have changed into a different kind of monster. The phony cool-boy type.

And as she was wondering this, she watched the dazzling Cheri Henderson, in her desk right across the aisle from Albert, turn to him and flash her sticky pink smile as they exchanged homework.

It was as if, on her stroll down memory lane, Opal had tripped and skinned her knee. All the hurt of that treacherous kiss, the kiss between Albert and Cheri, shot through her again. For a second she thought she might be sick. She closed her eyes and brought her hands to her throbbing forehead. Then, hiding her shame behind her hair, Opal hurriedly folded Albert's note back into its airplane shape. On its side, in heavy black lines, she scribbled a circle of her own. But instead of dotting the eyes and curving a smile, she scratched a jagged black lightning bolt across the O. Just like the logo on her tracksuit.

Air Opaline, she thought bitterly.

On her smartphone, she tweeked Albert a curt message:

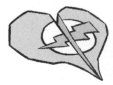

> From @onlyopaline to @albertfnumbers: Got
> ur note. Hav ur ansr. Incoming!!!

Albert felt his phone hum inside his secret pocket protector, right next to his heart. He fumbled to fish it out and check the text. Then, hopes high, he twisted around in his seat.

Opal met his puppy dog eyes. She could sense the milky clouds passing over her own, and she blinked to clear her vision. Albert grinned wider as she batted her lashes at him. Or so he thought! The, *ahem* . . . fool . . .

With a crisp jab of her wrist, Opal sent Albert's love note back into the air. Mr. Grates was facing the whiteboard, plotting a graph. But some of the other kids noticed and followed its flight path as it soared just below the diode lights. The plane peaked, then began to waft down toward Albert. He could make out the lightning-bolt *O* scrawled on its side. But just before he could catch it and read whatever Opaline had written back to him, something odd happened.

Seemingly out of a nowhere, like a live wire on the loose, a thin volt of electricity cracked across the classroom. It singed the crown of Brad Hochoquatro's afro and grazed Emma Appleby's raised hand before—*kzzzt!*—it hit its target.

The scorched paper airplane crumbled to pieces in Albert's grasp.

From behind his charred glasses, Albert sighed, more besotted than ever. So this is what it meant to be love-struck! He bet Opal's reply had been full of promise. Before some freak faulty wiring in the LEDs obliterated it!

Albert may still have had smoke in his eyes. But from where she sat, Iris's view was crystal clear. That was no faulty wiring, of course. It was Opal herself, shooting her trademark lightning bolt straight across the classroom.

Opal's not just mean, Iris thought, recalling Cheri's prediction about things getting worse. The girl's a fire hazard!

5

Welcome to the Club

"WE IN THE CLUB, THE PLACE BE PACKED, IF YOU'RE A UV then this is where it's at. Where my girls, where they at? The kids go crazy when the mutants get smacked!"

Behind the closed door of Iris's bedroom, Scarlet bounced on the bed. Her tutu hung low across her hips, gold doorknocker hoops swung from her ears, and Iris's rhinestone stylus took the place of a microphone in her hand.

"Scar, your English is atrocious!" Cheri declared from her spot on the carpet, where she was dusting her silver mani with a sequined pink topcoat. "And you already know where your girls are at—we be right here. I mean, we at right here. No, I mean, we *are*. Ooh, now you've got me doing it!"

"Sorry," Scarlet said sheepishly, getting down with her bad self from the bed. "I thought we should have a theme song for the Ultra Violet clubhouse. To go with the secret handshake dance!"

The girls had considered making the basement of the Jones's bluestone townhouse their hangout. But with three older brothers as well as her mom and dad, Scarlet worried about privacy. It was just Iris and her mother in the Tylers' mod apartment, which had a way more sparkly view. The glass-windowed wall of Iris's bedroom looked out across the spires and skyscrapers of Sync City. In one direction, the girls could see the HQT and its rock-crystal laboratory, the FLab. That was where Iris's mother—all three of their mothers—spent most of their time, experimenting. In the other direction, across the Joan River, stood the mucus-yellow Mall of No Returns—the place where BeauTek, right at that very minute, was probably manufacturing mutants. And who knew what kinds of weird makeup and creams! Even though the mall was not a pretty sight, the Ultra Violets had to keep an eye on it.

But it was the secret door that sealed the deal about the clubhouse.

What secret door, you ask?

Iris hadn't noticed it at first, either. Because it was hidden behind the big stuffed headboard of her bed. But the Sunday after the showdown at the Vi-Shush, she'd been dancing on her mattress, too. (Not superdancing, like Scarlet. Just dancing-dancing, Iris-style!) And when she went to nudge the bed back into place, she couldn't *quite* push it flat against the wall. There was a curious little lump in the patterned velvet wallpaper.

Being an artist, Iris was intrigued . . .

Being an artist, Iris had a sharp pair of scissors . . .

And long story short, with a snip here and a rip there, she had soon cut around the edges of a narrow door that had been covered up by the wallpaper. The pretty patterned damask was still in place. Iris just trimmed it off the doorknob. That was the lump. Kind of like the princess and the pea, if the pea were a doorknob and the princess had been sleeping standing up against the wall. So maybe not like the princess and the pea at all.

For such a modern building, the doorknob was oddly old-fashioned: a white ceramic oval with a spiky purple blossom painted on it. Even more odd was what Iris discovered behind it . . .

"Well, word up, my homegirls," she now said, squeezing

behind the big stuffed headboard of her bed and opening the door, "to CVUV!"

Bumping into each other as they got in line, Scarlet and Cheri burst into giggles.

"What's so funny?" Iris asked over her shoulder as she started up the spiral iron steps on the other side of the door.

"You said 'word up'!" Scarlet's snort circled through the stairwell.

"You called us"—Cheri could barely catch her breath—"'homegirls'!" Splaying her hands at her sides to keep from smudging her nails, and with Darth snuggled in the tote bag on her shoulder, she had to take the spiral steps extra slowly.

"Okay, fine!" Iris said as she parted the beaded curtain at the landing. "I'll leave the rapping to Scarlet."

"And to birthday presents," Cheri said with sudden seriousness as she slipped through the beaded strings after Scarlet. "It's always thoughtful to rap presents." Which only made Scarlet and Iris giggle all over again. Springing from a triple pirouette, Scarlet soared across the wide-open space.

"Club Very UV!" she belted out, and cannonballed into a shiny beanbag.

Iris, getting into the silly spirit, did a spontaneous handstand.

From her upside-down point of view, she thought she saw a dark figure dart past the windows, even though they were *many, many, many* stories up above the street.

A black swan? she wondered.

But when she cartwheeled right-side-up again, the twinkling towers of the skyline were all she could see.

It hadn't been long since Iris had stumbled across the secret door and discovered the small corner loft, and it still took the girls' breath away, it was so magical. The outer walls were carved entirely from clear rock crystal, same as the FLab. And the room jutted out at jagged angles into the air, like a giant rhinestone blossom that had sprouted right from the side of the sleek apartment building.

"It's like we're standing inside a flower!" Cheri had marveled.

"It has awesome acoustics!" Scarlet enthused. She was working up the courage to audition for the school musical and needed a place to practice where her brothers wouldn't tease her.

The room itself was almost empty when they'd found it. Just a few pieces of furniture had decorated the space: an egg-shaped swivel chair in a fuzzy orange fabric; a funny-looking sofa made up of lots and lots (and lots) of round white cushions, like marshmallows, pieced together on a slim steel frame; three wheeled stools; and, opposite the sharp petal window, an oblong black marble table.

Plus a shaggy pink fake fur rug in the middle.

The girls had no idea who the furniture had once belonged to, or how long it had been there. Based on the amount of dust they wiped off, it must have been decades.

To prettify the place, they'd strung the beaded curtain where the spiral staircase opened onto the floor. But the wrought-iron steps actually curled all the way to the ceiling. The first time Iris showed the room to Scarlet and Cheri, she worked up *her* courage, climbed to the top, and opened the hatch, popping her head out like a prairie dog. The high winds practically blew her corkscrews straight as she

checked out the roof. It was wide and flat. Just to the side of the hatch, a red light *blink-blink-blink*ed.

"That's for pilots," Scarlet had said knowingly. "And aeroscooterists and maybe even the Wonkavator. So that they see the tops of buildings in the dark."

The second time Iris climbed up there—with Scarlet keeping a firm grip on her ankle, and Cheri keeping a firm grip on Scarlet's ankle below her, and Darth wrapping his tail around Cheri's ankle at the bottom of the chain—Iris reached across and painted the blinking red lightbulb with a sheer blue wash.

And now the light flashed violet.

They could see it from inside, through the crystal of the ceiling. "It's our signature color!" Iris had beamed, pleased.

It hadn't been easy to get ol' Skeletony, the former FLab skeleton they'd rescued from the Vi-Shush, up that spiral staircase. And maybe okay definitely they'd bumped his bony skull once or twice, knocking loose a tooth or two. "Oopsie," Cheri had muttered as molars clattered like coins down the iron steps. Now Skeletony had a gappy grin to go with the citrine gemstone glinting from one eye socket. Cheri added a pink feather boa left over from some long-ago talent show. In the corner of the room, Skeletony cut a very dashing figure.

The beanbag from Scarlet's place had been less of a haul, since it was so squishy. She'd also scavenged strings of old holiday lights from her basement. When the girls turned them on, the inside of Club Very UV was almost as sparkly as the Sync City skyline. And positively more rainbow-bright!

All we need now, Iris thought, *is a mirror ball.* She was keeping an eye out for one.

On the marble table they propped their laptops or tablets and textbooks. Above it Iris had tacked their portraits—three blown-up smartphone photos she'd custom-colored. She'd made herself mostly purple, of course. A magenta glow surrounded Cheri's smiling face. And Scarlet shone with a rich eggplanty shade called aubergine.

There was still enough space on the wall for a portrait of Opaline.

Iris raced to the center of the pink fur rug. "Secret Handshake Dance!" she declared. Cheri and Scarlet rushed to join her, and they stood in a row. "Ultra Violets ready and—

> *"Pinkie touch, hair brush, twirl three times,*
> *bunny hop, cat claws, V's across your eyes!*
> *Shoulder shimmy, booty shake, twirl three times,*
> *catch the bus, catwalk, V's to the sky!"*

It was a very jazzy handshake. And Scarlet's first foray into choreography.

"Okay, Ultra Violets!" Iris said, pretzeling her legs beneath her as she dropped into the swiveling egg chair. "First order of business: Operation Get-O!"

5½*

Boys in Black
{*Halfsies Because Chapter 5 Was Already Too Long to Fit in This Part, Which Is Very Important}

"OPERATION GHETTO?" CHERI ECHOED, DRAPING herself diva-like across the marshmallow couch. "But I thought we were going to bring Opal back before we did any community service–type stuff."

"We are!" Iris nodded, her violet curls bobbing. "That's why it's called Operation Get-O!"

"Ohhhh," Scarlet said, getting it. Pumped from the handshake dance, she was freestyling in front of CVUV's massive flower window. Out of the corner of her eye, she thought she saw a couple of dark shapes swoosh by.

Two black swans?! she wondered.

"But what about the mutants?" she asked, turning her attention back to their plan. "Shouldn't we be trying to stop them?"

"I've thought about that, too," Iris said, twisting a grape ring pop on her finger. "But they go hand in hand—or claw, or tentacle, or whatever *ew* the mutants have." She shuddered.

"If we get Opal back on our side, it will help us control the mutants, right? They obey her every command!"

"True enough," Scarlet said, pointing her toe and circling her leg in *ronds de jambe*. "So how do we do it? Especially after our smackdown this morning!"

Cheri sighed. "I'd say we should fix her up with Albert, but alas!" To demonstrate her despair, she once again brought the back of her hand to her forehead. "We all know that equaled disaster *last* time I tried." From his comfy spot on top of the couch, Darth sighed, too, and swished the tip of his violet-striped tail up across his eyes.

Iris and Scarlet exchanged glances. Scar was tempted to make another joke about The Kiss That Changed Everything, but she concentrated on her *grands battements* instead.

"Albert does like Opal now, though," Iris said. "Did you see when he sent her that note in math this afternoon?"

"Yeah," Scarlet snickered. "And did you see the way she totally toasted it? That was hilarious."

"And kind of insane," Iris added, shoving off from the marble table to set the egg chair spinning. "It's crazy-dangerous for Opal to be running around Chronic Prep shooting off random lightning bolts. Remember what she said about taking over the class? Do you think she's going to start electrocuting students?"

"Oh *swell* no," Scarlet swore, crossing in front of the flower window in *chaîné* turns. "What that girl needs is an intervention."

"Exactly!" Iris exclaimed with a clap of her hands. "Genius idea, Scar!"

Still whirling, Scarlet asked, "Wait, what'd I say?"

"We'll stage an intervention!" Iris stated, grabbing her tablet to start jotting down the plan. "Maybe at Tom's Diner . . . ?"

"No, seriously?" Scarlet said, coming to a stop. Because she'd meant it kind of sarcastically.

"Isn't an intervention when everybody gets together and gangs up on you to tell you why you're so terrible?" Cheri mused, shifting sides on the marshmallow sofa. "That might backfire as badly as my Albert makeover."

Scarlet thought of all the reality TV shows her parents watched. "An intervention is like when people have too much junk in their garages and their family forces them to get rid of it."

Ring pop jutting out of her mouth, Iris frowned. "When you both put it that way . . ." she trailed off. "I guess I thought we three could just sit Opal down and talk things over. Find out why she hates us so much and try to fix it."

Cheri frowned next. "I've tried to tell her sorry about Albert so many times," she said, running a sequined hand through her hair, "but she just won't listen."

Scarlet frowned last. "I never did say sorry for always borrowing her lunch, but"—she couldn't resist another chance—"I didn't think that was as big a deal as sucking face with her crush."

If those marshmallow pillows hadn't been stuck to the sofa, Cher would have thrown one at Scar. The superdancer pressed a fist over her lips to hide her smirk.

"Hey!" Iris said, pushing herself off from the table for another spin. "Isn't Opal's birthday coming up? How 'bout we throw her a surprise party?"

Iris imagined balloons and streamers and ice-cream sandwiches, all in an Opal-esque color scheme of creamy vanilla, like her name, and dark chocolate, like her hair. *Sweet!*

Scarlet imagined smashing a piñata stuffed with bubblegum and press-on tattoos. *Score!*

Cheri imagined Darth in a tiny paper hat. *So cute!*

They all perked up instantly.

"A surprise birthday party intervention!" Cheri said, sitting up straight. "Maybe we can invite Albert. And those two boys at the window, too?"

?!?!?!?!

Just as Cheri was saying it, Scarlet gave Iris's chair a push with a tad too much *oomph*. She went careening toward the flower window, gripping tight to the fuzzy orange arms of the egg, her ring pop clenched between her teeth. With Scarlet *pas-de-bouréeing* behind her, Iris rolled right up to the window, pressing both palms against the panes. Plain as day she could see that the dark forms were not black swans at all. They were two boys in three-piece suits, hanging from bungee cords outside Club Very UV!

Scarlet came nose-to-nose with the shorter one, nothing but the glass between them. Her mouth dropped open and her freckles practically jumped off her face in shock. The boy had freckles of his own, across the bridge of his nose.

His mouth ran in a serious straight line above his square jaw. From underneath his crash helmet, tufts of salt-and-pepper hair stuck out. But Scarlet couldn't see his eyes, which were hidden behind black sunglasses. Suddenly he snapped a camera, and she staggered back from the flash.

The other boy wore black sunglasses, too. He was much bigger than his partner-in-spy: taller *and* broader. The straps of his bungee harness stretched thin under his weight. The buttons of his suit jacket strained across his stomach, threatening to pop. As Iris stared at him, she actually worried his cord might split and send him plummeting. Even if that would serve him right for spying!

He didn't take any pictures. He just balled his hand into a plump fist and shook it at Iris.

How rude!

Iris came to her senses and powered up quick. Fanning her fingers out in V's just like she'd done for the secret handshake dance, she whipped off two ultraviolet flares way too intense for mere sunglasses. The big boy raised his arms and the little one ducked his head as the sunbursts exploded

against the crystal window. Hoping they were temporarily blinded, Iris got to work painting a solid black curtain in the air. She concentrated hard, but it was taking a long time—the window was so wide! Shorty kept clicking his camera, aiming all over the place. Like a pro volleyball player, Scarlet jumped up to block his every shot. Finally, fumbling with their ropes, the Blob Boy fixed whatever had gotten them stuck in the first place. Crinkly carrot-red hair puffed up from his helmet as both boys dropped out of sight.

The whole scene had lasted seconds at most, but the girls were shaken.

"O . . . M . . . V," Cheri said slowly, approaching the window with Darth in her arms. "Two boys spying on us, and they weren't even cute."

Scarlet leaned her face against the cool windowpane, breathing hard. "The short one was, maybe," she panted. "But I'm still going to totally kick his butt when we catch them."

"We'd better report this to Candace," Iris said, abandoning her half-drawn black curtain and dashing to the table to video-call their erstwhile (*you know!*) babysitter. Scarlet, brimming with even more energy than usual, backflipped off the window. But she launched herself with so much strength that instead of a soft landing in the beanbag, she hit the wall ten feet above it. "Owie," she muttered as she slid down—although, in a weird way, pounding into the wall made her feel a bit better. Or at least calmer.

On Iris's tablet screen, Candace came into view, the camera angle warping her geek-chic glasses way out of proportion. Below her blunt baby bangs, her forehead loomed enormous (when it really wasn't).

"What's up, UVs?" she said in a low voice, looking over her shoulder to make sure none of their moms in the FLab noticed.

"Candace!" Iris gasped. On the other side of the computer, she probably looked all twisty, too, with big blue kewpie eyes and purple ringlets spiraling out in every direction. "We were planning Operation Get-O when we caught two boys bungee-spying on us!"

"Um, what?" Candace whispered, glancing over her shoulder again so that all Iris saw on the screen was the back of her head. And the stainless-steel teeth of the swizzle spork Candace almost always had in her hand. "You've been bungee jumping in the ghetto?"

Iris tried again. "No, Get-O!" she said. "A party intervention to win Opal back. And two boy spies in black!"

"Me and the protozoa will be *right there*!" Candace called, clearly NOT in response to Iris, before leaning in closer to the screen. "Probably not a good idea to throw a birthday party for spy boys," she advised. "You can't trust 'em."

"Spies, or boys?" Cheri asked, wheeling the fuzzy egg chair back to the table with Darth seated on its cushion, enjoying the ride.

"Huh?" Iris spluttered at the screen. "No, the party is for Opal. We—"

"Girls, we'll have to video-chat later," Candace cut her off. "The FLab's got a minor crisis on its hands, and the web is going nuts about some rumored olfactory weapon. It's all over PuffPo. Er, nothing to fret about, though!" she said, forcing a funhouse smile at the screen and reaching forward to fold it down. "I'll check my MAUVe cam footage for the spy kids. In the meantime, set the flower window to SHADY, okay? Coddington out!" was the last thing the girls heard.

"Oh, I forgot!" Iris keyed a code into her smartphone that instantly cast the club's windows in an eerie ultraviolet light. Candace could sometimes seem scatterbrained, but only because she always had a million different things on her mind. She actually was a total teenius, and between her and Cheri's supercomputer mind, they'd tricked out

CVUV with tons of hi-tech gizmos. So many that the girls hadn't memorized them all yet! When the window was programmed to SHADY, they could still see outside. But no one could see in.

"It's totally like you predicted, Cher," Iris said, erasing the curtain she'd painted with broad sweeps of her hand. "Black Swans. Two of them! We already have our work cut out for us with Opal's threats, and now some boys are spying on us, too?"

"I don't think they got much evidence." Scarlet rubbed her sore shoulder. "I think I blocked most of the shots."

"Awesome," Iris said. "It's ultra that you did that, Scar. But how did they find us? If we're not even safe in Club Very UV . . ."

Standing beneath her own portrait, Iris leaned back against the table, arms folded across her chest, chewing on the remains of her ring pop. From her beanbag crash pad, Scarlet anxiously punched the palm of her hand. Cheri broke the silence with a simple question:

"But the surprise party's still happening, right?"

Paint My Name, Paint My Name

OH, IT'S HAPPENING, ALRIGHTY. IT'S ALL HAPPENING.
The rise of O+2 at Chronic Prep. Opaline's ominous stench.
Bungee-jumping spy boys in black. Crisis mode at the FLab—
whatever that meant. And a city crawling with mutants. See?
Stuff happens, whether you want it to or not. But the Ultra
Violets passionately believed that there were few problems
in this crazy world that an ice-cream surprise party couldn't
solve. Even when that surprise party was doubling as a
birthday intervention to get their ex-bestie back from the
dark side.

Phase one of Operation Get-O found Iris hanging out
downtown on Saturday afternoon. This corner of the
city was known for its quaint cafés and bakeries, organic
vegetable markets, and gourmet food shops. All the top
chefs shopped there for the best ingredients, which is how
the neighborhood got its name: Kitchen Sync. Iris had been
taste-testing exotic ice-cream flavors for the past hour.

Now she was waiting for Scar and Cher to meet her so that she could share the results and they could all decide which would make the best sandwiches.

All those ice-cream samples hadn't completely soothed Iris's worries about O+2 and mutants and spy boys. But she was trying to stay hopeful about throwing Opal a party. And it was so exciting to explore a different part of Sync City! She'd even dressed up for the occasion. On her wrists she'd piled bunches of the beaded friendship bracelets she'd either made herself or traded with Scarlet and Cheri. A teensy blue heart-shaped sticker decorated one cheek. And on the ends of a few of her purple ringlets she'd fastened peacock feathers. Peeking out like a lace slip from beneath the lavender strands, the iridescent teal fringe looked viomazing.

Now, standing in front of the Gelato Be Chilling Me Ice Cream Shoppe, Iris breathed in the crisp air. It was perfumed with all sorts of yummy Kitchen Sync scents: cinnamon and saffron and star anise. She sighed with contentment, closed her eyes, and tried to forget all her troubles. All the aforementioned happening stuff. After an hour spent sampling ice cream, she was feeling even sweeter than usual, and for that fleeting moment life seemed delish. A breeze rustled through the fluffula trees, and it sounded like a whisper.

Like someone was whispering just to her.

Saying *Psst! Psst! Irisss!*

Iris's eyes fluttered open again, and she tucked a peacock-festooned curl behind her ear. Yes, there it was again, she hadn't imagined it! *Psst, psst, Irisss!*

Her UV radar on alert, she scanned the street. No, no sign of mutants. She scanned the sky. No, no sign of Candace's satellite MAUVe cam. And yet the whissspering persssisted!

Pssssssssst! Irisssss!

With hesitant steps, holding tight to the messenger bag strapped across her shoulder, Iris rounded the corner of the gelato shoppe and inched along the side wall. The whissspering grew more insissstent with every step, until she reached the back of the building.

Keeping super still, she peeked into the parking lot.

His back to her, a tall, skinny boy balanced on a hoverboard, tagging a battered dumpster. A threadbare black top hat poked out of his messenger bag. The frayed hem of a striped T-shirt hung above his jeans. He gave a vigorous shake to a can he was holding. *Pssst, psirissst!* went the spray-paint as he colored.

It was as if a thousand flavors of ice cream swirled together in Iris's stomach and all the sugar rushed to her head. She couldn't see the boy's face. But she just *knew*. It all came flashing back to her. That time in the monorail car. The daisies he'd painted. The funny wolfman she'd drawn with just her superpowers when he wasn't looking. The wolfman she'd drawn with a *top hat* . . .

OMV! Iris thought. Just then the boy hovered a bit to one side, and she could see what he'd spelled out in phat kaleidoscopic letters. It was Iris who whispered next.

"*Sebastian.*"

Hearing his name, the boy pivoted around. The top hat nearly toppled out of his bag and a shock of black hair fell across his forehead as their eyes met.

OMCV! Iris felt just like the ice cream she'd eaten. All melty inside. And totally frozen! She flattened herself against the side of the building, but she couldn't seem to move. Should she stay? Should she go? What would a true artist do? What should *she* do?

Such indecisiveness really was not like her.

Before she could ask herself any more questions, Graffiti Boy appeared before her, floating on his hoverboard like some hipster vision.

"Purple Girl!" His voice broke a bit as he spoke but was still as soft as the whispering spray paint. He cleared his throat, and his dark eyes were shining as he said, "So, now you know my name. What's yours?"

Iris's heart was beating so hard she was sure the teensy sticker was throbbing on her face! She opened her mouth to answer, and . . . nothing came out. Sebastian arched an eyebrow at her, confused. But Iris managed to smile. Her brain freeze eased a bit. She stepped out into the parking lot, toward his painting, her peacock feathers wafting behind her, and he followed. With a playful twirl of her pinkie finger, she silently asked him to turn around.

"Oh, okay," he said, getting her meaning (and maybe remembering their monorail paint-off, too?). "I'll close my eyes and count to ten."

Ten seconds didn't leave Iris much time! She powered up, the ultraviolet beams radiating through her—and surely burning off whatever remained of all that ice cream! Concentrating on the rusted dumpster, blinking her periwinkle blue eyes for just a second or three, she pictured three deep purple petals that had a touch of sunshine yellow on the inside. (Iris knew that her namesake flower was actually more complicated than that, but she only had ten seconds!)

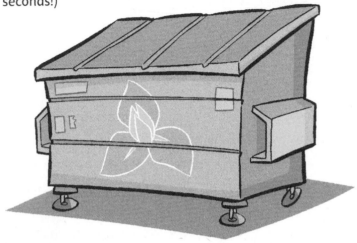

"Ready or not!" Sebastian warned, and spun around on his hoverboard again just as Iris was pretending to put her own (nonexistent) markers back in her messenger bag. "Hmmm," he said, eyeing the flower, then Iris. "Very pretty."

Iris blushed pink. Still, what were the chances that a hoverboarding graffiti boy would know—

"Iris!" he said with a snap of his fingers. "Is that it? Did I get it right?"

Iris smiled so bright she must have been blazing ultraviolet, but she couldn't help it. Sebastian flew a little closer, just above the ground, took out the tattered top hat,

and with the same gallant bow he'd given her in the monorail car, tipped it. "Cool to meet you again, Iris. At last."

He offered his hand. Trembling, she took it. When their fingers touched, he flinched, her skin was so warm. Holding his hand, Iris was finally ready to say something. Say anything! She gulped. He was the one on the hoverboard, but she felt like *she* was flying.

No, wait, she *was* flying. Or at least airborne?

"*Gelato be kidding me, RiRi!*" Scarlet growled in her ear. The pint-size Ultra Violet had picked up Iris and thrown her over her shoulder as if she were as light as her peacock feathers. Iris had been in such a graffiti ice-cream haze, she hadn't felt a thing! She never even noticed Scarlet and Cheri arriving in the lot behind the ice cream shop.

"*Iris!*" Cheri hissed in her other ear. "*You've got to hide your high beams! We could see flashes of rainbows from the street!*"

Just then, two more boys on hoverboards swooped in alongside Sebastian. "Yo, dude, we've gotta go!" one said urgently, glancing with almond-shaped eyes at the three intriguing girls. The other one revved the engine of his board and scratched nervously at what were really just the suggestions of scraggly sideburns. "Yeah, Sebastian, the minor crimes squad is scouring Kitchen Sync!" he explained.

"Toodles, then!" Cheri called to the boys with a flit of her fingers, too concerned about an increasingly neon Iris to flirt. "How perfect that the police are chasing you, because we really must dash, too, alas."

Iris, in a daze, still held tight to Sebastian's hand, so Cheri yanked her by the ankles like a rope in a tug-of-war while Scarlet pushed from the waist. "You know how it is, boys," Cheri continued. "Ice creams to choose, parties to plan, interventions to stage . . ."

"You're having a party?" the boy with the almond-shaped eyes blurted out. "Because I'm Malik—"

"Douglas!" the sideburned one introduced himself next.

"*Enchantée*, truly," Cheri said, because she *was* rather charmed to meet them. For vandals, they seemed like polite boys. "But we have to go now. *À bientôt!*" She added that last bit because she kind of *did* want to see them some other time.

The yelp of a police siren from the street cut short their chat. Scarlet and Cheri pulled Iris in one direction; Malik and Douglas pushed Sebastian to leave in the other.

But for a moment there in midair, Graffiti Boy and Purple Girl held hands. And as they each let go, Sebastian gripped one of Iris's bracelets and it slipped off her wrist.

She could still see him clutching it, fist to heart, as Scarlet carried her away.

Sweet and Vi-Shush

SASSAFRAS PISTACHIO, CHERI PONDERED AS SHE SKATED
home the following Sunday from her volunteer gig at Helter
Shelter, Sync City's haven for strays. *Caramel Raisin Rose.*
Because that was how she rolled. *Honey Blue-Blue, since Iris
hearts berries.* She was making a mental menu of ice-cream
flavors. *And Peach Melba, especially for Opaline . . .*

Cheri wondered what Darth's favorite flavor was. She'd
have to ask him. He was probably napping now up in CVUV.
Cheri couldn't very well bring a skunk to an animal shelter!

And she couldn't bring him home, either, because of her mom's allergies. But Iris would smuggle him back to her before school tomorrow. The thought of stroking his soft fur again and telling him all about her weekend actually made Cheri look forward to Mondays.

Slappity-slappity-slappity-slappity … A jogger with a bullfrog's wide mouth and webbed feet leaped past her, bringing a halt to her happy thoughts. "Ugh!" she shuddered, watching him go. "Mutants!" The last thing Cheri wanted to do was battle another army of them. If only they could beat the odds and get Opal back on their side, maybe they wouldn't have to.

Her apartment building was just a block away. But right as she reached her corner, Cheri's platform skates seemed to short-circuit. Sparks spat from the wheels, and with a staticky *zzzt!* she fizzled to a stop.

"Furi," she said, pulling out her smartphone by the woolly green bunny ears of its crocheted case, "reboot platform roller skates."

"I'm sorry," came Furi's clipped robotic response. "No can do, gurl. System Override."

"System Override?" Cheri repeated, staring down at her feet. "Skates, don't fail me now," she muttered. "I'm almost home!" She tried to upload the wheels back inside the platform heels so that she could at least walk the rest of the way, but the app wouldn't complete that function, either.

"System Override," Furi cyber-spoke again.

Cheri stuck out her lower lip and blew a random strand of auburn hair from her eyes. She debated whether she should take off her sandals altogether and go barefoot. To gauge the distance, she glanced toward her doorway. But when Cheri looked up, her supercomputer brain didn't just clock the precise mileage (10.4 yards, FYI). It locked onto a figure leaning there, waiting.

Little bolts of electricity fizzed from the girl's shoulders. Grinning at Cheri like some of the sneakier cats she knew, she raised a pinkie finger to her lips and blew on it like a smoking pistol.

"System Override, my eye," Cheri grumbled, carefully tiptoeing forward on her locked wheels. "Good thing Darth's safe back at Club Very!" But, her mind on her menu and her menu on her mind, she summoned up her cheeriest Cheriest bestie voice and called out, "Hi, Opaline! Here to see me?"

Oh, it was indeed awkward. Awkward indeed. Inward awkdeed, which doesn't even make sense, that's how tense it was! Cher had not had a civilized conversation with Opal since all the Albert drama went down. She didn't want to give anything away about the ice-cream sandwich intervention. But maybe this was her chance to soften Opal up.

Much to Cheri's surprise, Opal shot a smile back at her.

As long as Cher ignored the black lightning bolt zigzagging across her tracksuit, Opal almost looked the same as she had before she went electric. *When she was Opaline Unplugged*, Cheri wistfully recalled. She even thought she saw traces of her old friend in the warm brown of her eyes—until clouds of white roiled over them.

Cheri = wary.

Opal held out a lollipop. Which should have been nice of her, but just seemed weird, because that was what Iris always did. Cheri took the candy anyway and tried to smile. "Prune!" she noted. "Yum?" Remembering Opal's nasty Smashface slam, the pruney rumor she'd started about Iris, Cheri tucked the lollipop in her tote bag instead.

"I'll save it till after dinner," she said.

Then both girls just stood there for what felt like forever: Opal snap-crackle-and-popping with electric currents, Cheri's mind whirring with millions of possible outcomes of their encounter. And her nose wrinkling at Opal's faint but foul scent.

"So, Cher," Opal said at last. "I know I kind of lost it before over . . ." Opal paused to roll her eyes. Maybe she meant it as a way to bond with Cheri. But with her all-white sockets and voltage sizzling off her shoulders, she looked terrifying. " Albert Feinstein," Opal continued. "But boys come and go."

73

"Oh!" Cheri said, desperate to lighten the mood. "Are there boys coming, too?" She craned her neck to search past Opal down the street.

Opal screwed her lips into a twist, and for a second Cheri thought she heard thunder. But then Opal took a deep breath through her nose and unwound her mouth again.

"It's just an expression," she said drily. "What I meant was, we shouldn't let some nerd like Albert come between us when we have so much in common."

This is what Cheri had been trying to tell Opal all along! So why did she feel so doubtful now?

"Um, yes," Cheri agreed, calculating her next sentence extra carefully. "The four of us should definitely be besties again. I know Iris and Scarlet want that, too."

Opal narrowed her eyes so tightly her brows nearly met above her nose. Her stick-straight hair began to rise sideways. This time Cheri *definitely* heard thunder.

Once more, Opaline inhaled.

"You know," she said to Cheri, releasing her breath, "you don't really need the Ultra Violets. You could have even more, er, sparkly fun hanging out with me, BellaBritney, and Karyn. Bring that little skunk of yours along, too. O+2 could always *multiply* to O+3, right?"

Cheri was not liking that math.

Opal gave her a nudge. The spot where her elbow made contact felt like it had been Tasered. "After all," she asked a

74

vibrating Cheri, "didn't you used to hang out with Karyn all the time before Iris came back to Sync City?"

And before Karyn went all LIZARD! Cheri thought, aquiver. But she didn't say it, because she hadn't packed her polka-dot umbrella that morning. If Opal got any madder, she'd surely make it rain. "That was a long time ago," is what she said instead. "Before you came to Chronic Prep, too, Opaline!" She tried to toss in a lighthearted laugh at the end, like "ha ha ha!" But it came out all high-pitched and trilly, like "ha-he-eek?"

In a gesture so sudden it made Cheri jump, Opal raised both hands to her face. Then she began rubbing her temples, as if she had a headache. "Cher," she said in a low, flat tone, her head bowed. "*You* know, and *I* know, that you're different from Iris and Scarlet. One's a painter, the other's a dancer, big whoop. *You're* the one with the brains."

"Alas, 'tis true!" Cheri said with a heavy sigh, slouching against the opposite side of the doorway. "I can't deny it." She was still struggling to embrace her mathematic superpowers, and every morning she reminded herself it would be petty and ungracious to be jealous of her best friends' gifts. Even if, in her heart of hearts, she still sometimes wished the Heliotropium goo had given her the dancing superpower instead.

"No!" Opal snapped in frustration. A bolt of lightning sliced through the sky. "Don't you get it, Cheri? Your math brain is the best power of all! Who needs to draw a rainbow or dance a tango?"

Cheri shrugged. "I'd settle for a samba," she said, imagining herself in a fabulous feathered headdress.

"Cher . . ." Opal sounded irked. "The Vi-Shush—"

"The Vi-Shush!" Cheri cried out before Opal could say another word. "That horrible place?"

"It's not horrible!" Opal protested.

"They had bunnies in cages!" Cheri exclaimed. "They turned Darth Odor into a chemical weapon!"

"Exactly!" Opal shouted, clutching her head again as the gathering clouds clapped.

The first time the Ultra Violets had come together as a supergroup was when they stumbled across BeauTek's top-secret lab, the Vi-Shush, on level C of the Mall of No Returns. In an epic battle, the UVs had beaten Opal's army of mutants and freed the test monkeys. And Darth! As far as Cheri knew, Opal's mom still worked there.

"Listen, Cheri," Opal argued, her hair now fully

horizontal. "The Vi-Shush is doing lots of cutting-edge research! Not like the silly FLab, where all they do is, like, track missing socks! With me as a one-girl electric company and you as a math whiz on roller skates, just think what we could achieve!"

"What, Opal?" Cheri demanded, all the bestie friendliness gone from her voice. "What did you have in mind?"

Opal fell silent, and the two girls stared at each other. But now it was way beyond awkward. It was . . . raw.

"I thought I could reason with you." Opal rolled her white eyes again, like that had been the craziest idea ever. "But one way or another"—she glared at Cheri, and the thunder grumbled doomily as she spoke—"I'm going to change your mind."

The threat sent a chill through Cheri. And suddenly the scent of Opal's perfume seemed so overwhelming that she thought she might be sick. But she didn't show it. She just stared back at Opaline, past the milky white clouds to the warm brown underneath, desperately searching for the sweet, shy girl she once knew. The girl who blushed when she confessed her crush on Albert Feinstein. The girl who NEVER would have thought test bunnies were okay! Was she really gone for good? How could an ice-cream sandwich ever be enough to bring her back?

"Oh, Opes," Cheri said, sounding more sad than angry. "All I want to change now are my shoes." The encounter had depressed her completely, but she tried to salvage a smile. "See you tomorrow at school, okay?"

Without waiting for an answer, Cheri clomped into the lobby of her building on her locked roller skates. She could hear the rain as it started to fall, stabbing the sidewalk in thick liquid spears. But she didn't, she wouldn't, she refused to look back at Opaline. She didn't have to. She knew Opal was still standing there, stormy. The stench of her perfume crept out like grasping fingers, clinging to Cheri's clothes, to her hair.

The second I'm inside my apartment, she thought, *I'm taking a shower!*

Just as Cher started up the stairs, a thin white line of electricity snaked through the doorway and hit her wheels. They spun to life again. Cheri lost her bearing on the bottom step. She flailed. And her smartphone crunched in her back pocket as she landed on her butt. The crocheted bunny ears didn't do much to break her fall.

"Platform Roller Skate System Restored," Furi reported in her tinny voice. "And owie, you are sitting on me."

Uninvited

"IN A WORLD WHERE CHEERLEADERS HAVE SPLIT personalities and trendoids have tails . . ."

Iris did this thing where she introduced their lunch periods like movie trailers. At first she had just pretended to film the cafeteria through the frame of her fingers. But then she started recording the little videos on her smartphone.

"In a world where your lab partner just might be a mutant . . ." she continued in a mock voiceover, panning across the room.

"How come, in trailers, it's always 'in a world'?" Scarlet wondered, flipping open her brother's hand-me-down Batman lunchbox with so much force that it bounced back off the tabletop, nearly catching her fingers. "Where else would it be? It's got to be in some world or another, doesn't it?" She unwrapped her sandwich. Tuna fish again. She wished her mom would change it up a bit.

Iris swung the lens around, zooming in on Scarlet.

"Sometimes," she said, echoing Scarlet's comments, "in some world or another, the secret of life can be found . . ."

Scarlet held up half her lunch ". . . in a sandwich!" she chirped with a wide fake smile, tossing her head so that her ponytail whipped around as she worked the camera.

"And *scene!*" Iris clicked off her phone and sat down at the table. "Sync City Pictures presents *Eat, Yay, Fudge: The Almost True Story of an Ice-Cream Sandwich Intervention.* Scar, very persuasive. All your acting practice is really paying off!"

Cheri managed a smile. She'd sort of told Iris and Scarlet about the awkward-slash-scary-slash-depressing-slash stinky encounter with Opal yesterday afternoon. But not really. Scarlet was so obsessed with her upcoming audition for the school play, and Iris so into planning the surprise birthday party, that Cheri didn't want to rain on their sundaes the same way Opal had rained on hers. Even if, after Opal's latest storm, the forecast was cloudy with a chance of evil.

Cheri was a vegetarian, but she'd take a chance of meatballs over evil any day of the week.

The girls were going to e-mail everyone right after school, with a big "*Shhh! Surprise!*" in the subject line. Next to her lunch tray, Iris turned on her tablet and opened their guest list. At the very bottom, in swirly letters surrounded by stars and hearts and question marks, she had written with her rhinestone stylus:

Sebastian+2?!

"Sebastian plus two?" Scarlet read upside down off the screen. "Graffiti Boy and the other two skater punks?"

"Malik," Cheri said, remembering their names. "And Douglas."

"Iris," Scarlet said sternly, "I don't think you should see Sebastian again if you're going to go all rainbow! We can't let anyone know about our powers, remember? And what do we even know about those boys? What if they're spies like the Black Swans?"

Iris just stirred her straw in her blueberry juice and sighed.

"Gosh, I hope not, but Scar's right, RiRi," Cheri agreed with reluctance. She believed in all kinds of star-crossed love, be it mouse-elephant, chocolate–peanut butter, or Lucy-Schroeder. But the Ultra Violets absolutely, posismurfly could not risk revealing their powers. "Rainbows are a no-no. And all your other pretty colors, too."

Iris sighed again, a faraway look on her face. Then, to tease her two friends, she asked, "You mean colors like these?" And she flashed through a slideshow of patterns, her face quick-changing from rainbow stripes to polka dots to camo before returning to normal. "Anyway, how would I even find him again?" she said, thinking back for the trillionth time to Sebastian floating on his hoverboard, clutching her bracelet to his chest.

Unbeknownst to Iris, Cheri had already developed a Sebastian algorithm—a bunch of steps that, if followed, she was sure *would* lead to Graffiti Boy sooner or later, even in a place as big as Sync City. She'd run all the outcomes in her brain. But nuh-uh, Cheri was not about to say so, oh swell no. Between Iris's uncontrollable rainbow outbursts, Scarlet forgetting her own strength, and Opaline threatening electrical storms, Cheri wasn't sure *what* to do anymore. She sat silently at the lunch table, chewing on a celery stick and contemplating a chip in her manicure. In her bag on her lap, Darth nibbled on a slice of celery, too.

With a sudden shake of her curls, Iris snapped out of her daydream. "Oh well, whatever, never mind!" she said. "Boys come and go, right?" She didn't sound very convinced. It was more of a question than a statement. But Cheri still sat bolt upright: Opal had said the exact same thing!

"And," Iris went on, "we already have a different 'plus two' to deal with."

All three UVs turned their attention to the other side of the cafeteria.

Opaline was holding court in Nerdsville. Or what used to be Nerdsville. The girls didn't know what to call it anymore. Before, in yet another combo of star-crossed opposites, the nerds sat next to—but never with—all the popular kids in the outpost of the cafeteria known as Trendster Nation. But now the two groups were mixed together like chocolate chips in cookie dough. The social networks had been stirred up. That should have been a good thing, the in-crowd chilling with the geeks and vice versa. It *should* have been . . .

So why was the vibe in the cafeteria so Debbie Downer?

Nobody seemed to be laughing much, or gossiping. Girls weren't gathered together around their phone screens, texting or posting on their Smashface pages. Jocks weren't playing catch with defenseless pieces of fruit. A few students on the fringes had their noses in their notebooks, finishing up assignments before the afternoon classes. Others were just holding their noses, trying not to inhale the potent pong of brussels sprout sweat socks emanating from Opal's corner. The whole cafeteria was so quiet, they may as well have been in the library.

Cheri scanned the ceiling for any sign of clouds.

"Don't worry!" Iris whispered, a twinkle in her eyes. "Our ice-cream surprise party is going to cheer everyone up! By this time tomorrow, the cafeteria will be on a sugar high!"

"Hope so," Scarlet said with a smirk, nodding back toward Trendnerd territory. "Because that is just *sad.*"

Albert sat at the far end of the table, gazing adoringly at Opaline. His mouth hung open above his laptop keyboard. "O-M-faux pas," Cheri muttered. "If he drools, that would be *very* not cool." After her makeover, the boy should have known better.

"Sad," Scarlet repeated. "And strange."

At the other end, next to Opal, K-Liz was eating cheese ravioli, the special of the day. Every now and then she'd bow her head and stab her forked tongue into the pasta squares. Cheer Britney stood beside her, kicking one leg and rustling her solitary pompom. Goth Bella ignored her rah-rah half, reciting phrases of dark poetry instead. Put together, it sounded a little something like this:

"Quoth the raven, *gggo* team!"

That is, it sounded utterly confusing.

85

Iris frowned at the sheer weirdness of it all. Scarlet had to laugh.

"A cheerleader shouting Edgar Allan Poe," she said, shaking her head and swinging her feet under her chair. "Hilarious!" She swung so high her foot hit the table, lifting it off the floor. It came clunking down again. "Oops!" she blurted out, grabbing a napkin to mop up the juice she'd spilled before it could reach Iris's tablet.

"And you stress about me and my public rainbows," Iris chided her.

"Sorry," Scarlet said with a sheepish grin. "Still getting a grip on the superstrength thing."

Cheri just looked from one girl to the other, masking her worry with another weak smile. Sensing her tension, Darth pawed up at her, then nuzzled his head into her hand.

Keepz kalm an sparkel on, he told her.

It was a solid motto. It made her feel a bit better.

The bell rang. "Already?" Iris exclaimed, tucking her tablet into her messenger bag and chugging down her cup-o-soup.

"Time flies when you're *not* having fun, I guess," Scarlet tossed in, looking again at all the glum students. She rushed to finish her lunch and gather up her books, too. But all three UVs stopped what they were doing when they noticed the peculiar procession passing them by.

With BellaBritney semi-cheering in the middle and K-Liz bringing up the rear, Opaline marched out of the cafeteria. "O+2!" she commanded, swooping her arm in a circle with two sharp snaps of her fingers. As other students trailed behind, dragging their feet like they were headed toward final exams and not just another Monday afternoon, a sheet of paper slipped from someone's open backpack. The swish of K-Liz's tail sent it skimming across the linoleum floor.

Iris bent down to pick it up. Scar and Cher gathered around. So you could say they all got the bad news at the same time.

"*By invitation only . . .*" Cheri read the printout. "*You'll be SHOCKED, but it's true . . .*"

"*Opaline is turning the Big 1-2 . . .*" Scarlet continued.

"*Be there if you know what's good for you,*" Iris finished.

The date for the party was, of course, Opal's birthday: the very same date of their surprise.

The three girls exchanged glances. Then Scarlet snatched the paper out of Iris's hand and scanned the top, reading down the names of everyone else in their class. "Nope!" She gave a rueful laugh. "We're not there!"

"Check out the PS," Iris said, pointing to the bottom of the page. As if they needed further proof.

PS. If ur name is Iris, Scarlet, or Cheri, go suck on a lollipop bcuz u r NOT invited!

"*Quelle* rudeness!" Cheri gasped. To be a social outcast was upsetting enough, but to be blown off by a bestie? Okay, a *former* bestie, but one they were trying to make up with? One they'd been planning an ice-cream intervention for!

"So much for our surprise party," Iris said softly. "Guess the real surprise is on us."

Scarlet was so agitated, she spun three pirouettes right there in the middle of the empty cafeteria. "Yeah," she stopped for a second to say, "and now we're stuck with a whole gallon of Peach Melba!"

The Outsiders

IRIS HAD NOT FORGOTTEN WHAT IT WAS LIKE TO BE AN
outsider. After all, she had moved away from SynchroniCity
when she was only seven, leaving her three best friends and
everything she'd ever known behind. Then she spent the
next four years at astronaut offspring boarding school while
her mom was lost in space. And when she finally returned,
Iris had to cope with everyone at Chronic Prep freaking out
over her wild violet hair.

So Iris was used to being on the fringes. And tougher
than you might think, considering she was usually all peace,
love, and lollipops on the outside.

Scarlet was tough stuff, too. That was no secret. If
anything, she had softened up a bit since Iris had come back
to Sync City, and she'd starting hanging out with Cheri again,
and she'd become a superdancer. (Which *was* a secret.) Still,
just a sideways glance from those steel-gray eyes and a boy
twice her size would run screaming, clutching his waistband

in panic. Such was Scarlet's reputation for pantsing bullies.

But Cheri . . . It was she who was taking the snub by Opaline the hardest—alas! (As she would say.) Cheri had always been naturally popular—so popular she never gave it a second thought. All the kids liked her, trendoids and geeks and jocks and goths and any clique in between. Because what wasn't there to like? Fabulous, funny by accident, wouldn't hurt a fly: Cheri got invited to every birthday party, and her social calendar was always jam-packed.

Until now.

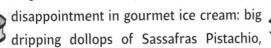

The girls had already tried drowning their disappointment in gourmet ice cream: big dripping dollops of Sassafras Pistachio, Caramel Raisin Rose, Honey Blue-Blue, and, yes, Peach Melba, squished between chocolate-chunk cookies or crispy butter waffle wafers. After three

sandwiches apiece, they were feeling a little better. And a little ill.

They agreed to donate the remains of their ice-cream stockpile to Scarlet's three older brothers. They left it where they'd stored it, in Scarlet's basement freezer.

Now the Ultra Violets were hanging out atop the grassy knoll in Chrysalis Park. Cheri's dad had urged her to get some fresh air, saying it would "shake her out of her glumdrums." Iris's mom was working at the FLab, as usual. And Scarlet had SO much energy to burn, her parents didn't mind one bit about the ice-cream binge. They were just glad their little spitfire daughter was playing in the park instead of sitting in detention.

Scarlet hadn't gotten detention in weeks!

Her parents didn't know that Scarlet had found a much more deserving target of her righteous anger: mutants. Schoolyard bullies were child's play compared to the evil threat that was BeauTek. Of course, Scarlet still wouldn't hesitate to put a bully in his or her place. It was just, between homework and being a superhero and practicing for her audition, she had a lot on her plate.

It was a beautiful afternoon. Wherever Opal was, she must have taken the clouds with her. The sun shone bright in the pure blue sky. Iris lifted her face to it, soaking up its warmth. Then she flopped down onto the park bench and slung an arm around Cheri's shoulders.

"Try not to be too sad, Cher," she said, giving her a squeeze. "No matter what happens with Opal, you've always got me and Scar. And Candace."

"And Darth," Scarlet added. "He's hopelessly devoted to you!" She jumped, bending one knee while extending the other leg straight out behind her in a jazz stag leap. Springing about in the grass like that, she really did look like a tiny, ponytailed deer. In a tutu.

"I know," Cheri said, combing her retro red fingernails through Darth's silky fur. "It's impossible to be friends with Opal when she's acting all über–mean girl, anyway. But I do wonder . . ."

Cheri trailed off, gazing past Iris to the darker blue of the Joan River. Iris couldn't help noticing that Cheri's normally bright green eyes seemed a little darker, too.

"What?" Scarlet prompted, poised in a straight-leg scorpion pose.

Cheri blinked twice before continuing. "Well, is this

what it's always going to be like," she said quietly, "being a superhero? Hiding who we really are, forever?"

Iris and Scarlet were silent. They had both thought about it, as well. Keeping their secret—from the other kids at school, from their teachers and parents—that was hard, but they could do it. Cheri was talking about something else. About loneliness.

"I wonder about that, too," Iris replied at last, giving her a second squeeze. "I mean, my mom has always been oblivious, even before my purple hair. But how could I ever be a hundred percent honest with, you know, um"—her cheeks reddened as she said it—"Sebastian, or any other boy, if I always have to lie to him about being an Ultra Violet?"

"Just don't have boyfriends, I guess?" Scarlet said, switching to split-leg calypso leaps. Though that didn't seem to be a satisfying answer. Not even to her.

Iris sprung to her feet, suddenly restless. "We'll figure it out," she said, smacking her fist into her open palm, determined. "We have to! Okay, Operation Get-O completely derailed, but we've got to find out what's up with this 'shocking' party of Opal's."

"That we're not invited to," Cheri groused, because she still couldn't quite believe it.

"And there's still the mutant situation," Iris continued. She turned toward the river, and her pupils shrunk to pinpoints at the sight of the acid-yellow Mall of No Returns on the other side. "If mutants overrun Sync City, then nobody gets to have boyfriends. Not even 'the oblivios.'"

Cheri sighed. "Sometimes I miss being an oblivio," she admitted. "Things were so much simpler then."

"Maybe," said Scarlet. This depressing convo was making her restless, too. "But if I were still oblivious, I wouldn't be able to do this."

With a great burst of energy, Scarlet flipped backward, rising twenty feet off the ground. Midair, upside-down, she vogued her arms around, then landed in a split on the grass.

Iris grinned. Cheri could feel her radiant heat and see the pale violet light glowing from her hands, her hair, her eyes. "And *I* wouldn't be able to do this!" Iris said. With a wave of her fingers, she drew out the branches of the single fluffula tree till they arched over the hilltop like a frilly fedora hat. For an extra-special touch, she changed the color of the leaves to peppermint swirl. Then did a swirl herself underneath the

candy-striped canopy she'd
painted on air. Rainbows
beamed from her fingertips,
filtering out through the leaves.

"And *I* . . . " Cheri announced
with a little skip off the bench,
unable to resist the minty freshness,
". . . couldn't, um, calculate the square
root of pi!"

"Pie rules!" Scarlet shouted, jumping up with a fist pump,
her hand shooting through a scrim of leaves that
weren't really there.

U no couldz heer me too, Darth reminded
Cheri with a nudge.

"Or hear sweet little animals,"
she said, hugging Darth close. "Even
though I'd talk to them anyway." She
smiled for the first time that day.

The sounds of flapping and
crashing caught all three of them by
surprise. Scarlet shot up from her split. Iris
erased the pretend peppermint leaves. And Cheri kept the
square root of pi to herself. With the fluffula tree pruned
back down to actual size, the girls were stunned to see what
had caused the commotion.

"The Black Swans!" Scarlet gasped.

Boys Come and Go

HAPLESSLY HANGING BEFORE THEM ONCE MORE WERE the two spy boys in their black suits and shades. Big Red had snagged his jacket collar on a tree branch, while Lil' Freckles was upside down, his ankles wrapped in the straps of his binoculars.

"Binoculars?!" Scarlet shouted, stamping her foot. She hit the ground so hard, rivulets of dirt avalanched down the grassy knoll. "And is that a *camera* AGAIN?"

She was so mad, it never occurred to her to be embarrassed. Even if Lil' Freckles looked a lil' adorable, all topsy-turvy and helpless, she refused to notice. She stomped right up to Big Red and wrestled the camera out of his sweaty hands.

It crunched like a candy wrapper in her fist.

"Oh, oopsie," she muttered, forgetting her own strength as usual. "Didn't mean to crush it," she started to apologize. "Or did I?!" she yelled, remembering again that they were SPIES. She gave Big Red a push—jus' a lil' one—in his jelly belly, and he swung back and forth from the tree branch like the piñata they'd bought for their ice-cream party fail.

"Hey!" he cried. "Stop it—that's an order!"

Scarlet gave him another shove—this one a lil' less lil'. "Do I *look* like a waitress?" she snapped

Iris and Cheri fanned out behind Scarlet. Iris had a mind to melt the sunglasses right off those boys, but she couldn't risk revealing her powers. What had they already seen?

"Who are you?" she demanded instead. "What do you want?"

Though they were clearly sitting ducks—or sitting black

swans—trapped as they were in the tree, neither boy broke the code of silence.

"Give it up, Lil' Freckles," Scarlet snarled, her own freckles flaring on her cheeks. She folded her arms across her chest. "Or do you want to find out what an upside-down wedgie feels like?"

Lil' Freckles folded his arms upside down right back. "We're well aware. Of your wedgie skills. Miss Jones," he said through gritted teeth. "And your propensity for pantsing. It's all. In your file."

"*My file?!*" Scarlet exclaimed with another ground-shaking foot stomp.

"And do not. Call me. Lil' Freckles," he warned. His voice was so strained, the girls wondered if his lunch was backing upside down on him. "I am contractually due. For a major. Growth spurt!"

"Then maybe we should call you Overdue Spurt instead!" Scarlet scoffed. The thing about the file was freaking her out, but she wasn't about to show it. She twisted her fists together, preparing to deliver the kind of wedgie she was famous for. Apparently!

"No!" Big Red cracked first. "Upside-down wedgies are in violation of the Universal Anti-Bullying Convention!"

"That'll never hold up in front of any student council!" Iris countered, jumping to Scarlet's defense. "Not if you're caught spying!"

"Who said anything about spying?" Big Red jeered. As he spun in the breeze, his voice petered off in different directions like a wind chime. "We were just, uh . . . bird-watching. From up in this tree."

"Bird. Watching," Lil' Freckles repeated, all constipated-sounding and rat-a-tat terse. "It's. A free. Park."

The Ultra Violets exchanged glances. Obviously the spies were lying—hello, the file? Scarlet was enraged. Iris was irate. And Cheri was smiling.

Cher's dad had always told her she could catch more flies with honey. She'd just never wanted to catch (ew) flies. But now that the tree had caught these spies, she figured, *Close enough!*

She approached the dastardly dangling duo, Darth still in her arms. His purple-striped tail draped over the crook of her elbow. "Bird-watching, hmm?" she drawled, rocking the skunk like a baby. "That sounds like so much fun. Maybe the five of us should have a playdate," she suggested sweetly, "*if you ever get down from that tree.*" Then her voice dropped as she delivered her sugarcoated demand. "Now unless you'd prefer a face full of skunk stink, tell us what you saw."

Stubbornly, Lil' Freckles still held his ground. (That's another expression. He was really still in the air. His arms were still folded, and behind his dark glasses, he was still staring at Scarlet.) But Big Red wavered, his eyes on Darth and his hands clapped over his nose. "Er," he squawked, "we're not sure—"

"Agent Bristow!" Lil' Freckles barked.

Big Red ignored his partner.

"I know it sounds crazy," he said, "but it looked like a crow in a red dress—"

Scarlet scowled. "Quoth the raven, I don't think so," she muttered under her breath.

"—followed by a spinning purple flamingo."

Iris kept a straight face. "That's the most ridiculous thing we've ever heard!" she said, tossing her hair over her shoulder. Then she blasted two laser-thin, laser-quick, undetectable ultraviolet beams at the lil' one's binocular lenses, warping them. Just in case the goggles had a built-in camera, too.

"I know, right?" Big Red said. "And we couldn't really see because it was like the sky was filled with peppermints all of a sudden! It's how we lost our balance in the tree. All that swirling made us dizzy."

"A peppermint sky." Scarlet traced her toe *en dedans* in

the dirt. "Sounds like you've been hitting the cough syrup a little too hard there, Red," she said, winking at Iris.

"Agent Bristow!" Freckles bellowed again. (He had a loud voice for such a lil' fellow.) "Keep. It. Together! You know the punishment for snitching!"

"What, Baxter, what?!" To the Ultra Violets' complete surprise, Big Red began to cry. Like a lil' baby. Plump teardrops dribbled down from behind his dark glasses. The girls feared a snot stream would snot be far behind. "They shredded our camera, dude." He let out a hiccupy sob. "We've got zero intel! We're stuck in a friggin' fluffula tree. The nice one's packing a *skunk*. And that chick in the tutu scares me!"

Scarlet had to bite the inside of her cheek to keep from smirking. First she was a crow, now she was a chick? These Black Swans were for the birds!

Iris beckoned the girls close. Cheri placed Darth on the ground as guard, tail locked and loaded, before joining the huddle.

"Okay," Iris said, keeping one eye on the captives. "The bad news is, they're totally spies. This whole crying game has got to be an act—like, good spy–bad spy. The good news is, we destroyed the evidence."

"High five!" Cheri whispered, and the girls slapped hands down low.

"But now what?" Scarlet hissed. "Should we take them prisoner? I carry the big one, you two share the Lil' Spurt?"

Iris and Cheri looked at her, astonished.

"I don't know!" Scarlet said. "We could keep them in my basement. Feed them Peach Melba on crackers!"

"Yeah, because what your mom needs is two *more* boys in the house," Iris joked, and all three girls burst into giggles in spite of themselves.

From where the two agents hung on the tree, those girly giggles were more unnerving than the wedgie threat.

"No, let's set them free," Iris said when she caught her breath. After their serious convo and intense spy-boy interrogation, it felt good to laugh. "We can't ask them about BeauTek without giving away that we know about it, too. Hopefully they don't know what they saw. We've got their names now—Bristow and Baxter. And maybe Candace has been tracking them by satellite MAUVe cam."

In agreement, the girls touched pinkie fingers, then straightened up out of the clutch.

"We have it on good authority," Cheri called to the thwarted spies as she picked Darth up off the ground, "that boys come and go."

"So before we spray you with a sample of our skunk's newest perfume . . ." Iris said, twirling a purple ringlet around her finger.

"You. Should just. Go!" Scarlet shouted.

By now, Big Red was a big wreck. He had gotten his sobbing under control, but he panted and pawed at the air like a paddling dog. The tree branch bent with his weight. Lil' Freckles did the talking for both of them.

"We'll agree not to question you further," he said, "if you'll just"—he cleared his throat—"get us down from this tree." Then his face flushed tomato-red. Either he was completely embarrassed, or all the blood had finally rushed to his head.

The Ultra Violets stood there wondering how, in fact, they would free the spy boys *without* using their superpowers when they heard the low hum of a hybrid motor.

"Iris! It's, like, fate!"

Floating behind them were Sebastian and his punky hoverboard posse.

If it was possible, the Black Swans turned an even brighter shade of tomato. With his suit cuff, Big Red tried to wipe the tears from his cheeks.

"Oh, hi, um, hi!" Iris said, hoping her hair looked all right. Inside, her heart was butterflying. But she could feel Scar and Cher staring at her. And after the close call with the spy boys, she concentrated on keeping cool. "What are you guys doing here?" she asked. At least this time she could speak! "How did you find us?"

Sebastian grinned, running a hand through the forelock of black hair that always fell in front of his eyes. Iris could see her bracelet on his wrist. *OMV, do not beam, no one must know, do not beam!* she repeated to herself.

"I saw a rainbow and followed it," Sebastian said in that same soft voice as before. "It seems like, wherever you go, there are rainbows." Then he smiled even wider, like he couldn't believe what he was saying. His buddy with the sideburns punched him on the shoulder, but Sebastian never lost his balance on his hoverboard.

Donotbeamnoonemustknow- donotbeam! Iris screamed inside her head. Out of the corner of her eye, she could see the UVs. Scarlet's eyes were wide with alarm. *"No!"* Cheri mouthed—*she* wasn't surprised one bit to see Sebastian there. It was the third scenario in her mental algorithm.

"What's up with these two in the tree?" Malik, the almond-eyed hoverboy, interrupted. "You guys all go to Chronic Prep, right? I guess you play some *strange* schoolyard games . . ."

"Oh, no, we don't know these boys, either," Cheri said, acting innocent. "We just came across them."

"They said they were bird-watching," Scarlet added. Her back to the hoverboys, she rubbed her hands together at the spies like she was fixing to pants them. Then she narrowed her eyes at Big Red.

"Dudes, help a brother out!" he yelped. "Get us down!"

Lil' Freckles put his hands over his sunglasses over his eyes and shook his head in shame.

"Would you?" Iris asked, flitting her gaze back and forth at Sebastian. She was afraid to look at him for too long. And dying to look at him for hours. She could feel her temperature rising and was sure she was going to break out in rainbows any second now. She couldn't let him know about her superpowers. About the painting, the camouflage, the ultraviolet rays. She couldn't let him know that she *was* the rainbow!

She had to get out of there.

"Yes, would you?" Scarlet repeated, then did her best impression of Cher. "Those great big boys are way too heavy for us *lil'* girls to lift!" she said, dragging out the *lil'* as long as she could.

"But that time we saw you behind the ice cream shoppe," Douglas, the hoverboy with the hint of facial hair, began, "weren't you the one carrying—"

"I said they're too heavy!" Scarlet silenced him with another tremorous stamp of her foot.

"No worries," Sebastian said, speaking only to Iris. His buddies zoomed over to the tree and began to unhook Lil' Freckles. "And then maybe after we could—"

"I've got to go now!" Iris blurted out. The low end of the color spectrum, the reds and oranges, were already throbbing from her fingertips. "So much homework!" she fibbed—and poorly, she was sure. At a loss for words once more, she leaned forward on her tiptoes and gave Sebastian a kiss on the cheek. "I'm sorry," she whispered, lowering her eyelids to hide the ultraviolet.

Then she ran down the grassy knoll, aiming her erupting rainbows into the dandelions and clover so that he wouldn't see them.

No One Must Know

"AND THAT'S WHEN WE SAW THE BLACK SWANS!"

Scarlet paused at this point in her story (*which, BTW, is also our story*) to quaff a slug from her mug of butterbeer. All this talking was making her thirsty. (*You too? Go ahead and grab a drink of water, then. It's okay. We'll wait.*

waiting

waiting some more

Back now?

Back to it!)

"The Black Swans, huh?" Candace muttered, peering down her nose through her big black-framed glasses as she scrolled through screens on her smartphone. "Cool. Did they play an all-ages show at the pier or something? I would have thought they were too rhythm-and-bluesy, too old schoolsy, for you girls."

Scarlet looked across the table at Cheri.

Cheri flared out her plaid pink fingernails in a shrug. Iris poked Candace in the shoulder with the long swizzle spork that came with her triple berry parfait. (Candace had left her own spork back at the FLab, so as not to arouse suspicion at Tom's Diner. From whence that original spork had come. From where, you ask? From whence!)

"Candace, are you even listening?" Iris wondered aloud. The girls were used to Candace being a tad absent-minded in a professory way, but that afternoon she seemed more distracted than usual. "The Black Swans are not a band!"

"They're a theory. About unpredictable phenomena," Cheri explained helpfully. "And ballerinas?" she added, turning back to the Ultra Violets' official superdancer.

"They're *spies*!" Scarlet hissed with such urgency that the foam flew off the top of her butterbeer.

Candace snapped her head up from her phone screen and her glasses slid down farther, past the tip of her nose to the top of her lip, where they sat like a plastic mustache. "Gotcha," she said, her glasses bopping as she spoke. "The spy boys." She squinted, stealing another glance at her phone. "Remember I told you not to trust them? Cute as they may look in their three-piece suits."

"We didn't!" Scarlet protested, banging her tankard on the table so hard she heard the glass crack. "And they don't!" She couldn't speak for Iris, who practically broke out in rainbows at the mere mention of Graffiti Sebastian. And Cher seemed almost above the charms of boys. But Scarlet herself would *never* let one get in the way of their supermission. Even if that sullen, stubborn Lil' Freckles was stil' a lil' on her mind. Hanging upside down from the fluffula tree like a holiday ornament, *he'd* never cracked. While his right-side-up partner had squealed like a pig! *So respect, Frecks, respect.* She had to give the lil' guy that much.

Scarlet's thoughts were interrupted by a towering column of hair. She immediately covered the mouth of her glass with her hands.

"Everything peachy here, girls?" their waitress asked, cocking an eyebrow at Scarlet. The white streak in her bride-of-Frankenstein beehive inched up above it. "You pounding that mug for a refill, hon?"

"Thanks, but we're good," Candace answered for the

table. As she spoke, her glasses fell farther still, and she had to catch them in her teeth to keep them from splashing into her tea. "Just having an animated conversation," she explained, her jaw clenched. The waitress's beehive loomed over her like a giant blurry Oreo.

"Moms, if you're that hungry, let me bring you a menu," the waitress said, pivoting on her orthopedic sneakers and heading back to the counter. "Don't go eating your glasses. They'll give ya indigestion."

Candace spit out her spectacles. "Why does she always think I'm your mom?" she said, wiping the lenses on her lap. Then she looked in the general direction of Cheri and winked. "How would that math add up?"

The girls smiled. Candace was the only grown-up (well, almost grown-up) they could talk to about their superpowers. Tapping into her connections at the Fascination Laboratory—the place from whence (*from whence!*) the life-altering, power-activating Heliotropium goo had come—she had promised to protect them, no matter what. She'd also promised to help them save Opaline from the dark side. The last time they'd been at Tom's Diner, Opal had been with them.

Now her space in the red vinyl booth sat empty, like a mouth that was missing a tooth.

But the UVs couldn't dwell on that today. They only had a few more minutes before Candace had to report for her job assisting their actual mothers at the FLab. So they picked up their discussion right after the beehived waitress dropped off a menu at the table.

"The Black Swans said they had a file on Scarlet," Iris explained, opening the menu and peeking out over it. "They knew about her history of pantsing!"

Scarlet's reputation for pantsing was kind of legendary, and Candace had heard about it plenty. At the FLab, Dr. Jones was forever complaining about the detentions her daughter received because of her aggressive behavior. "Well, we've all got skeletons in our closets, don't we?" Candace said, thumbing through screens on her smartphone again.

Cheri stopped midsip of her strawberry milkshake. "We keep Skeletony out in the open in Club Very UV," she said. "He makes a great decorative accent. And coat rack."

Candace considered this. "You're right, Cher," she said, putting her phone down and reaching across the table for some sugar. Or so she thought. "Sooner or later, closeted skeletons have a way of coming out." Then she poured what was really a packet of black pepper into her chamomile tea. As the girls looked on, curious, she borrowed Iris's swizzle spork and gave it a stir. "And if these Black Swans have a file on Scarlet, they most likely have files on you two, too."

It was a sobering thought. Iris tugged on a ringlet. Cher chewed on a thumbnail. And Scarlet tossed back the rest of her butterbeer in one gulp.

"At least they don't know what they saw," Iris said, trying to think positive.

"They thought we were birds." Scarlet twirled a finger round and round at her temple. "Cuckoo!"

"And Scar crushed their camera," Cheri added.

Scarlet frowned.

"Well, you did," Cheri said.

"It was an accident," Scarlet grumbled.

"A happy one," Candace interjected, "if that camera had pictures of you girls getting superfreaky on it." She ran a hand through her hair, and her blunt bangs stood up like a picket fence across her forehead. "Remember," she said, lowering her voice and leaning across the table, "you three are scientific wonders. We still don't know what's going on at the Mall of No Returns' mutant factory, and now these boys are spying on you. They could be from the government—"

Scarlet's mind filled with images of secret agents probing them like aliens.

"Or the military," Candace continued.

Iris flashed back to her years at boarding school and shuddered.

"So *no one* must know about your powers," Candace stressed. Then she took a sip of her tea and began coughing violently. "Spicy!" she croaked as an explanation, grabbing Cheri's untouched glass of water instead.

Iris sighed deeply, her eyes brimming watery blue. It didn't take a teenius to figure out what she was thinking. But as it happens, Candace *was* a teenius. And as ever, she had been keeping track of her three supercharges by satellite. By Miniature Aerial Unmanned Vehicle, to be exact. Or MAUVe, to be brief. Like an eye in the sky, the homemade camera drone tracked the girls. Candace just had to log on to the secret frequency she'd set up to see their (almost) every move.

"Iris," she said gently, clearing her throat and pushing her peppered tea aside. "I know you're crushing hard on that hoverboy with the top hat . . ."

Iris looked up at Candace, blinking back her tears.

"But if every time you see him you start glowing like a spaceship—"

"Overdue spurt." Iris cut her off with a shake of her purple curls, changing the subject. "That's what the short spy said, right?"

Scarlet nodded vigorously. "He said he was *contractually* due to grow."

"Remember the creepy Build-a-Girl Workshop on level

A of the mall?" Iris said, putting the pieces together. "I bet BeauTek can Tall-a-Boy, too!"

"Excellent deductive reasoning," Candace said, letting the topic of Sebastian drop. If she knew the girls at all, she knew she could count on Iris. "Sounds like those Black Swans have signed a contract with BeauTek. Maybe in exchange for a lil' nip-tuck? I'll do some research"—she peered at her phone for the umpteenth time—"see what I can find out. And if you run into them again . . ."

The UVs sat up straight, awaiting instructions.

"Admit nothing. Deny everything. Make counter-accusations. And see what else you can find out." Candace tilted her head toward Scarlet. "*Without* resorting to wedgies."

"By any means necessary!" Scarlet said in her own defense.

At that moment, the beehived waitress returned to the table and refilled Scarlet's butterbeer. "On the house, kiddo," she said between snaps of her gum.

"Er, peachy," Scarlet replied, embarrassed. "Thank you?" She'd already had enough of the sweet brew, but she guzzled more down right away. She could see the crack she'd knocked into the glass now and was afraid the syrupy amber liquid would seep all over their table.

"I'll take the check, please," Candace said, adding to the girls, "I've got to get to the FLab."

"Moms," the waitress griped good-naturedly as she tore their bill off her notepad and slapped it on the table. "Don't be in a rush to get flab. In my experience, it gets you!"

To make her point, she gave her rubbery butt a slap, then sashayed away, swinging her hips.

"That waitress is *très* weird," Cheri said, eyeing the bill. "But we should still tip her. Three dollars and sixty cents—twenty percent."

"What's up at the FLab, anyway, Candace?" Iris asked, scraping out the last bits of her berry parfait with a grape lollipop. Her swizzle spork seemed to have disappeared from the table.

"Yeth, whath's on your smarthphone that's more faschinating than our shtory about being *shpied on*?" Scarlet asked, her tongue thick with a coating of butterbeer caramel.

Candace looked around the booth at their three open faces. "I'm so proud of you guys," she said. "I know it hasn't been easy adjusting to life as secret middle-school superheroes."

"Thanks, Candace." Cheri accepted the compliment. "But you didn't answer the question."

"Right again, Cher," Candace said. "I didn't. Because I don't want to add more stuff to what you're already dealing with."

The girls sat up even straighter. At precise ninety-degree angles to their seats, Cheri could have calculated. Scarlet arched both hands above her head in fifth position.

"What more stuff?" Iris dared to ask, the stick of her grape lollipop jutting out of her mouth.

Candace picked up the swizzle spork (*ah, there it is!*) as she'd done many times before. She held it aloft as a warning, to keep them from speaking. "Big Red and Lil' Frecks may not be the only spies," she said. Then she sneezed—a side effect of the pepper.

"Gesund-wha?!" Scarlet whispered, ignoring the swizzle spork of silence and sweeping her arms down.

Candace waited a moment more, debating whether to tell them. But she knew knowledge was power: She couldn't leave the UVs in the dark. "I've been checking a hidden camera," she said grimly. "Someone's been sabotaging the FLab."

The Theater of Hard Knocks

NOT PEACHY.

That's what everything was. Unpeachable. The opposite of peachy. The anti-peach. Muchas gracias, beehived waitress, but no amount of butterbeer refills could quench the Ultra Violets' worries.

The next day, in the back of the auditorium, Iris pulled up the list she'd scribbled on her tablet, and slid down in her seat. Which had recycled hemp cushions, because Chronic Prep was a very eco-conscious school. Beside Iris in the dimly lit theater, Cheri and Darth did the same. Cher scanned the computer's screen:

> *YAY!*
> 1. We r superheroes.
> 2. We have secret powers and a cool super-group name.
> 3. And a swella cute skunk mascot.

4. And an awesome clubhouse!!!

5. Candace has our back.

6. Iris + Sebastian = tru luv 4evs?

MEH . . .

1. Opaline = still on dark side. ☹

2. Opaline = leading evil threesome w/LAME name.

3. Ice-cream intervention = #epicfail.

4. BeauTek = scary mutant factory, WTV?! ☠

5. Black Swans spying on us!

6. Someone sabotajing FLab—why?!

7. Midterm exams in 2 weeks, ugh.

8. Can never tell Sebastian my tru identity.

"Hmmm," Cheri hmmed. Even negating the Sebastian points—which didn't quite belong on ALL the Ultra Violets' lists of pros and cons—things did not line up. "I hate when the odds are never in our favor," she said.

"Me too!" Iris put the tablet back in her messenger bag and passed a black cherry lollipop to Cher. "That's why I think we have to double-down now, with a two-pronged approach."

"That's a lot of twos for the three of us," Cheri counted. "What do you mean?"

Iris propped her wedge sandals on the seatback in front of her. "One," she said in a low voice, unwrapping a blueberry lolly for herself, "we catch the Black Swans in the act and find out what their deal is with BeauTek."

"Totes," Cher agreed.

"And two," Iris continued, "we figure out what is up with Opaline and the birthday party."

"That we're not invited to." It had been a couple of days now since that newsflash, but Cheri was still not over the dis.

Iris turned to Cher. In the shadowy auditorium, Cheri thought she saw an ultraviolet twinkle in her eye.

"Just because we're not invited," Iris whispered with a smile, "doesn't mean we can't go."

"Oh!" Cheri breathed, surprised. "UV party crashers?!" She smiled back. Iris had been a bit wobbly recently, stressed out as she was over Sebastian. And Cher still believed in love against the odds, even be it of the supergirl–clueless boy variety. But she decided now was NOT the moment to tell Iris that she and Scar had given Sebastian her number that afternoon in Chrysalis Park, after she had run away on the verge of rainbowing. To see

Iris back in take-charge mode made Cheri feel more confident, too. She didn't want to do anything to upset the equilibrium (*which is a mathy word for "balance"*).

Instead, Cheri began imagining their party-crasher outfits. They would be way more glam than the spy boys' bland black business suits if she had anything to say about it!

Sumting smelz rotten . . .

Darth had scampered up to Cheri's shoulder and was sniffing the air.

"Huh," Cheri said, "I think Darth is picking up a scent."

Smelz sad, he told Cheri.

"Hey." Iris nudged her. "Speak of the Opal."

Opaline had just entered the auditorium. Trailing behind her, as usual, was BellaBritney, looking typically hip-hip-booray, and K-Liz, whose reptilian eyes widened as they adjusted to the dim light. Opal and K-Liz slipped into seats toward the front. BellaBritney cartwheeled out of sight.

"Do you think she saw us?" Cheri asked. "Should you go camo, blend in with the hemp?"

"Nah," Iris said. "We have just as much right to be here as she does. And remember what Candace said: Unless it's an emergency, no busting out our powers in public."

"Right," Cheri said with a single nod. She sometimes forgot, since all her superpowers were hidden in her head, anyway. "Let's just observe them."

P.U. Darth thought, covering his nose with his paws.

Just then the drama teacher, Ms. von Smith, strode across the stage in a cloud of gauzy scarves and billowing skirts. (Ms. von Smith was also the art teacher, and Iris's favorite.) She handed a sheet of paper to a boy sitting at the piano, who placed it on the easel above the keys. Then she walked to the front of the stage. Tucked her clipboard under one arm. Lifted her skirts as if she were about to jump over a puddle. And jumped off the stage instead. She could have just walked down the three steps to the side. But hopping off Poppins-style was definitely more dramatic. Ms. von Smith was all about the drama. Whether an audience was watching or not.

The teacher took a seat in the center of the very first row.

Auditions for the school musical were about to begin.

Iris and Cheri sat mostly patiently, slouched down in their chairs, sometimes texting or making half-hearted attempts to read their history homework while one student after another came out on the stage. Some kids were really talented, with strong voices. Others were decent dancers. The girls felt like they were behind-the-scenes judges of a singing competition, and they made a game of rating the performances in fake British accents. Until one name made them inch up in their seats.

And it wasn't the name they were waiting for.

"BellaBritney Bettenscourt," Ms. von Smith called in her high soprano. "You're next."

"*She's* auditioning?" Cheri muttered, astonished.

"For how many roles?" Iris wondered.

The girls giggled, waiting for BellaBritney to take the stage. Down in front, Ms. von Smith was waiting, too. She tapped her long fingernails on her clipboard. "BellaBritney Bettenscourt!" she spoke-sung again.

All the way back in their seats, Iris and Cheri could hear whispering from backstage. It sounded like two girls having a heated argument with each other. Or make that one girl having a heated argument with herself. At last Cheer B appeared, single pompom in hand, dragging her other half along. Goth B pulled the green velvet curtain with her, all the way out to the middle of the stage.

Ms. von Smith eyed the odd scene of the cheerleader clutching the curtain. She didn't say anything, just made a note on her clipboard. Then she nodded to the boy at the piano. "Okay, Sam," she said.

And he began to play.

Hearing her cue, Cheer Britney opened her mouth to sing.

"*The sun'll come out,*" she began, in what really was more of a shout. "*Gimme a* T*! Gimme an* O*! Gimme an* M-O-R-R-O-W*!*"

"Bet your bottom dollar that it *won't,*" came a surly voice from behind the curtain.

"*Just thinkin' about,*" Cheer Britney carried on with a shake of her solitary pompom, "T-O-M-*ORROW!*"

"Fills my head with cobwebs and completely crushes my soul," Goth Bella deadpanned, peering out at last. She was wearing half a black turtleneck and half a black beret. Cheri thought it might make a whole good party-crasher costume. But for the role of Little Orphan Annie?

"Fashion disaster," she murmured to Iris.

"I hope Scar's not so nervous that she's not watching," Iris murmured back. "Because this is totally her kind of train wreck."

"Er, thank you, BellaBritney!" Ms. von Smith clapped briskly, putting an early end to the confused audition. "A very, ah, *unique* take on the role of Little Orphan Annie. Very, ah . . ." The teacher searched for the right word. "Deconstructionist!" she declared, relieved to have found it. "The way you pushed past Annie's surface optimism to expose the real *pain* at the heart of her life as a poor street urchin. Bravo! I applaud your artistic bravery." And she clapped briskly again.

"Does that mean I got the *P-A-R-T*?" Cheer B asked, half of her bouncing with excitement.

"Oh swell no," Ms. von Smith said bluntly.

"Boo," Cheer B pouted, her lonely pompom drooping in disappointment. "Told ya," Goth B snarked. "Gimme an *L* and what does it spell? Loser!"

BellaBritney exited the stage, her cheer half ripping the beret off her goth half, her goth half pulling Cheer's single ponytail.

Watching from behind, Iris saw Ms. von Smith's shoulders shudder, which set off a chain reaction of tremors through her gauzy scarves. The teacher flipped up the page on her clipboard, then held it out under the lights as if she couldn't trust her eyes.

"Also auditioning for the role of Little Orphan Annie," she read out at last, "Scarlet Louise Jones?"

"Here!"

With a flying leap, Scarlet bounded from the wings. She was

carrying a tin bucket in one hand, and she sprung so high she just missed knocking out a spotlight with the mop in the other. She landed in a *plié*, then straightened up and straightened out her tutu. To make her audition more believable, she was wearing a white shirt collar on top of her rock-n-roll T-shirt—Iris had crafted it from a clean coffee filter using ribbon and scissors and glue. Cher and Iris had also spent the half hour before in the girls' room, coiling up Scarlet's licorice-stick strands with a curling iron. She might have looked like an especially tough Little Orphan Annie, except that BellaBritney had already claimed the title of Most Strange.

"Good energy there, Scarlet," Ms. von Smith said. "And I like the props. But let's wait for the music before we start dancing, shall we?"

Scarlet just nodded, gripping the bucket handle so tight that her knuckles turned white.

"You can do it, Scar!" Iris whispered, way in the back of the auditorium, where only Cheri could hear her. Cher and Darth sent Scarlet their most positive thoughts, too.

Ms. von Smith sized up the small girl before her on the stage. Scarlet Jones was known more for pounding bullies than pounding the boards. But school plays were excellent places for spirited children to channel their impulses, and the arts teacher totally believed in the therapeutic power of "the *theatre*." (If you could have heard her think it, you would have heard her pronounce it with an extra syllable and trill the *R*, like *thee-ay-tarr!* Most dramatically!)

The teacher gathered up her gauzy scarves and tossed them over her shoulder.

"The second song, is it, Scarlet?" she asked, settling back in her seat.

Scarlet nodded vigorously again, her black curls already coming loose.

"All right then, break a leg!" Ms. von Smith said.

"Whose?" Scarlet asked. She scanned the near-empty auditorium. Opaline sat with her arms folded a few rows behind the teacher. K-Liz flicked her forked tongue out at her.

"No, no, no," Ms. von Smith said hurriedly, "that's just an old thespian expression." Without explaining any further, she pointed to Sam at the piano. He flipped over the sheet music, then tinkled the keys.

Iris and Cheri linked pinkie fingers in anticipation. Scarlet had made them pinkie swear NOT to clap or cheer or scream or whoot or do anything that might distract her. So they both just held their breath and held up their smartphones. The screens scintillated with a sparkler app.

Scarlet's throat felt dry. That leg-breaking saying had broken her concentration, and she could see Opaline glowering in the audience. The piano introduction came and went, and the auditorium fell silent.

"Play it again, Sam," Ms. von Smith instructed.

And he did.

And this time Scarlet found her voice.

"*It's the hard-knock life*," she began quietly, "*for us . . .*"

Ms. von Smith smiled, surprised at how clear and pure she sounded. Scarlet saw that smile and raised her voice a little louder.

"*It's the hard-knock life, for us!*"

Iris and Cheri jumped to their feet and waved their phones.

"*Steada treated*," Scarlet sung out, loud enough to reach the rafters, "*we get tricked!*" She stomped her mop on the stage. It broke through the floorboards.

"*Steada kisses, we get kicked!*" She booted the bucket for effect. Her foot bent right through the tin, leaving a sneaker-shaped dent.

But Scarlet didn't really notice this. There on the stage, with the piano playing and the drama teacher toe-tapping along, Scarlet forgot everything else—her nervousness and silly hair and, of course, her superstrength, which she was always forgetting anyway. She burst into a viomazing hip-hop dance solo, creating her own rhythm section with the bucket and broomstick.

"*I'm from the school of the hard knocks, I must not*," she sang, suddenly switching to the rap version of the song, "*let mutants violate our blocks . . .*" The piano player got into it, too. He bounced up from his bench to beatbox along.

Sulking in the audience, Opaline began to shoot bolts above Scarlet's head. With each stage light she hit, the bulb would pop and shower down sparks. Still Scarlet sang, dancing between the electric raindrops, sweeping them up with her prop mop, spinning so fast that just maybe she was creating sparks of her own. MC-ing, freestyling, slapping the bucket like a bongo, she *owned* that stage. As she reached the end of the song—

"*It's!*"—she tossed the bucket to one side, and it soared all the way up into the balcony.

"*The!*"—she threw the mop to the other, and it speared through the green curtain, pinning it against the wall.

"*Hard-knock life!*"—she flung her arms wide open and slid forward on her knees just as Opal blew out the last of the stage lights. Its yellow embers twinkled down through Scarlet's fingers like falling fireworks.

From the back of the auditorium, Iris made a quickie exception to Candace's no-powers-in-public rule. She busted out a glitter-dusted beam, shining a cool lavender spotlight on Scarlet. She and Cher didn't have roses to sling at the stage. But Darth busted out his superpower, too, spraying the air with the sweet, powdery scent of violets.

Up in front, Ms. von Smith watched, rapt, as Scarlet sprang to her feet and gave her a crisp curtsy. The teacher was suddenly overcome by the heady smell of flowers. Perhaps she'd overdone it with her perfume that morning? It must have been making her giddy now. Because it appeared as if Scarlet Louise Jones's glossy black hair glowed with a halo of deep, dark purple.

What's the Deal?

SCARLET WAS STILL HUMMING TO HERSELF AS IRIS AND Cheri joined her backstage. She was still dancing, too. But then again, Scarlet was always dancing.

"OMV, Scar, you were so good!" Cheri gushed.

"Viomazing!" Iris declared. "Even dancing in the dark!" She spun around herself, violet curls flying, as the girls left the auditorium. "You'd make the most awesome Annie ever!"

Scarlet didn't know what to do with all the compliments. She searched the hallway for a bully to beat on, but they'd all already gone home. She considered giving Cher a friendly shove in the shoulder, then resisted the urge. She slapped her own shoulder instead.

"Owie," she laughed as they reached their lockers.

"What did you do that for?" Cheri asked, laughing too, while taking a cautionary step to the side.

"IDK." Scarlet shrugged, wrestling her history textbook out of her locker and cramming it into her backpack. "I just . . ." How could she explain this? "You know how people say, 'Pinch me, I must be dreaming'?"

"Yeah?"

"It's like that," Scarlet said. "But supersized. I have a lot of energy, I guess."

Iris reached over to rub Scar's shoulder where she'd smacked it. "Well, I bet you get the lead, and then you'll have to rehearse so much you'll be exhausted!"

"Hope so." Scarlet bowed her head to hide her smile. By now her hair was back to stick-straight and licorice-black. "Because most of the time it seems like . . ." She looked up from under her long bangs, first to Iris, then to Cheri. "Like the more energy I burn, the more energy I have."

"Oh totally," Cheri said, rummaging in her tote bag for her lip gloss, which was hidden beneath Darth's soft, snoozing belly. "Energy begets energy. Aha!" She dug out the tube of glittery plum and had begun to twist off its cap when she realized Scarlet and Iris were staring at her. "Energy equals mass times speed squared times the constant one half?" she tried. As if that were any clearer! "No? Okay, how about: A body in motion stays in motion," she attempted. "Scarlet, once your body is in motion, you're pure energy!"

Iris started twirling around them again. "You mean once

she gets started, she can't, she won't, and she don't stop!" she exclaimed, grasping it.

"She's kinetic," Cheri stated, rolling the gloss over the bow of her lip, then dotting it on the bottom.

Scarlet shut her locker and the girls continued toward Chronic Prep's revolving doors, chatting and laughing, spinning and explaining energy equations. But suddenly Iris held up a hand, and all three girls came to a halt. A few classrooms ahead, a shadow had darkened their path. They heard a door swing open, and as it did a wedge of conversation slipped out into the corridor. A funny jumble of a phrase:

"Five card draw, high hand wins."

Iris tucked a ringlet behind one ear and cocked her head to the side, listening. Curious, she took another step forward. That's when all three of them saw K-Liz slither across the hallway, her scaly tail swaying behind her as she snuck into . . .

"The boys' room?!" Scarlet gasped, clamping a hand over her mouth. Cheri made an automatic ick-face.

"Wow." Iris stuck out her tongue in an ick-face of her own. "I knew Karyn had gone mutant, but I didn't think she'd changed *that* much."

"Oh swell no," Scarlet said through her fingers, shaking her head.

"Well, something's going down in those toilets," Iris decided. "I wonder what . . ."

The girls had just about reached the boys' room when the door creaked open again. A cluster of kids, both boys and girls, stumbled into the corridor and scattered in different directions.

"I'm completely cleaned out," one complained. "That's my lunch money for the whole week!"

Another teetered toward the girls: Martin Gibbs, though they almost didn't recognize him at first. A milky film dulled his eyes, and his mouth hung slack. He seemed to be grasping at the air in front of him, reaching for something that wasn't there.

"Hi, Martin," Cheri said tentatively as he approached.

"*MMNOH!*" He gave a loud moan, swiping at her as he passed.

Scarlet immediately put up her dukes, and Iris instinctively raised a hand, too, ready to shoot out a burning solar ray. But the Ultra Violets held their fire as Martin just kept shuffling on.

"What was *that* about?" Cheri exclaimed, watching him go.

He smeld, Darth thought sleepily, still deep in his nap.

A couple more kids escaped from the boys' room, and this time Iris caught the door before it closed. Cheri and Scarlet bunched up behind her, Cheri peering over one shoulder, Scarlet peeking under the other. All three Ultra Violets dared to stare into the mysterious void that was the

boys' lavatory. And all three Ultra Violets wrinkled their noses in sync at the acrid ammonia stench of urinal cakes—topped with a faint but distinct scent note that could only be described as brussels sprout sweat socks.

"Quoth the raven, 'barf,'" Scarlet rasped, pinching her nostrils.

On the tiled floor of the bathroom, a motley mix of students sat in a circle. In its center was a small pile of stuff: chocolate bars, dollar bills, loose change, earrings, a Magic Eight Ball, someone's inhaler, three jelly pens, a ginormous rhinestone Hello Kitty ring. That kind of stuff. More kids surrounded the circle, leaning against the sinks and the stall doors. Cheri noticed Julie and Emma both checking their hair in the mirror. Scarlet narrowed her gaze at Duncan Murdoch, the horn-headed bully she'd wrangled with before. On the windowsill, backlit by late afternoon sun that gave the entire room a smoky atmosphere, sat Opaline. When she caught sight of the Ultra Violets, stacked like faces on a totem pole in the doorway, she began to slow-clap.

"Why look," she said, elbowing a glum BellaBritney at her side, "if it isn't Orphan in a Tutu. Way to copy my collar, Scarlet. *So* unoriginal." She gave a haughty sniff.

Scarlet could feel her cheeks start to flame. She'd forgotten to take off the flimsy coffee-filter collar Iris had made specially for her audition. Opal's collar today was studded with fat black pearls that gleamed above the lightning bolt on her tracksuit—totally glam in comparison. But a collar was a collar. Scarlet didn't know what to say.

"Spare us the sarcastic clapping, Opaline," Iris retorted for her. "Everybody knows Little Orphan Annie wears a collar. It's not like you invented them!"

"The style dates back to France at the turn of the last century," Cheri piped in. Math may have been her superpower, but she'd learned her fashion history all by herself.

"Hey, guess what?" a boy kneeling on the floor interrupted. "No one cares!" He pushed a gray fedora back on his head to glare up at the quarreling girls. "Shut the bathroom door already!" he hissed, tugging at the knot of his thin tie to loosen it. "This is a *secret* poker game, duh. If you dames ain't in"—he hitched his thumb—"get out."

Scarlet glanced at Iris, still embarrassed about the paper collar that she couldn't take off now, not with everyone watching. Iris scanned the scene; then her eyes met Cheri's with a question. Cheri cased the place before nodding in reply. The cards from the last round of the game lay face-up on the floor tiles. Her brain began to buzz as numbers and symbols flooded it: red hearts and diamonds, black clubs and spades, jacks, kings, and queens. Images of all fifty-two cards in a deck spread out like a patchwork quilt in her mind.

"Deal me in," Cheri said. And she sat down in the circle as Scarlet and Iris stepped inside the boys' room, their backs against the door.

13³/₄*

Poke Her Face
{*Because 'Twas Impossible to Fit a Whole Poker Game into One Chapter}

"ACES," FEDORA BOY SAID, TIPPING HIS HAT FORWARD again. With slick fingers, he gathered up the cards and began to shuffle the deck. "As I was saying," he announced to the crowd, "five card draw, high hand wins, joker's wild."

Hearing that, Cheri immediately added two jokers to her mental patchwork card quilt.

Fedora Boy flicked out five cards to each player, facedown on the floor.

Cheri picked up her hand and took a peek at it: Queen of hearts. Three of clubs. Ten of hearts. Five of diamonds. Eight of hearts.

Iz good! Darth said, poking his head out of the tote bag to take a peek, too.

Cheri discreetly rearranged her cards in numerical order. Her mind was racing, but she kept her expression blank so that none of the other players could read it. *If I can just get two other heart cards*, she thought, *I could win.*

Jax n' ninez, Darth thought back, his whiskers twitching, *an u haz flush!*

Considering they were sitting on the floor of the boys' bathroom, it took extra concentration for Cher not to make another ick-face at the mention of flushing. *And just how would a little skunk know that?* she asked Darth.

Lotz ov pokr in da joint, Darth explained, recalling his days caged up with monkeys and bunnies in BeauTek's Vi-Shush lab.

As soon as Fedora Boy had dealt out all the hands, two players groaned and folded on the spot, throwing down their cards in disgust and quitting the game.

Amachurz, Darth snickered.

In professional poker games, players are never supposed to show their hands, not even after they've lost.

Amateurs? Cheri repeated. *I guess so, but it's lucky for us they are!* She gave Darth a tiny tap on the nose, gently nudging him back down into his bag. *So no more snickering. You might make me laugh!*

She scanned the tossed hands to see if either of the cards she needed was among them. She didn't think so. On the imaginary patchwork quilt in her mind, she struck a line through those discarded cards and through the ones she already held. As her superbrain calculated all the remaining combinations, she held her five cards like a fan. Hiding behind it, she skirted her eyes at the other players. To the left of the dealer, K-Liz riveted her reptilian glare, reviewing her own cards while Opal shifted on the windowsill behind her, rubbernecking over her shoulder. And to her right . . .

"Mr. Grates?!" Cheri stammered, unable to keep her poker face straight at the sight of her math teacher.

"Miss Henderson," he greeted one of his best students, then noisily cleared his throat. "Nothing wrong with a little game of cards to let off steam after a long day of school," he said.

"Nothing at all," Cheri agreed nonchalantly, although she was pretty sure there was plenty wrong with it. As the teacher studied his five cards, she noticed the tan line circling his wrist like a pale tattoo. Then she glanced at the pile of prizes between them. A gold watch lay beneath the Hello Kitty bling ring.

"Draw," K-Liz was saying, and the game got serious, with the remaining players discarding the cards they didn't need and Fedora Boy dealing them new ones from the deck. Rounds passed, bets got bigger, and tension in the boys' room grew, till the only sound to be heard was the trickle of a dripping toilet behind one of the stall doors.

Beknownst to Darth alone, Cheri had drawn the nine of hearts she needed. To up her bets, Iris had emptied her messenger bag of lollipops. Cheri had tossed her pink polka dot umbrella onto the pile. K-Liz, to stay in the game, had wagered a bottle of sunscreen. Opal smirked at the sight of it, and Iris arched an eyebrow. Sunscreen: Was it really part of Opal's whole "O+2" scheme, meant to block UV rays? Or was K-Liz just trying to treat her scaly skin condition?

Mr. Grates broke the silence with a heavy sigh. He'd already given up his wristwatch, as well as a highly valued teacher's edition of the class workbook—the one with all the answers in red. He had nothing left to bet. And as he looked from K-Liz's squinty reptilian slits to Cheri's cool green gaze, he hadn't a clue which girl might be bluffing. "Bad enough I'm old," he said, in his usual style of nerdy rapping. "Now I've got to fold." He threw his cards down and quit the game, adding, "At least my watch isn't solid gold."

Opaline rolled her eyes at the ridiculous teacher. "Let's up the stakes," she said to the room, unbuttoning the black pearl-encrusted collar from her neck. "Cher, I know how

much you live for all that
glitters," she taunted, waving it
back and forth, its polished beads
glinting in the bathroom mirrors.
"And Scarlet's obvi desperate to
copy my style . . ."

Scarlet scowled across the
bathroom. Maybe Cher had to keep a straight poker face.
But Scarlet itched to poke Opaline in her face!

"So I'll throw my collar in for Karyn," Opaline challenged,
holding it up like a prizefighter's belt for all the kids to gawk
at. "If Cheri bets the skunk."

"You've got a skunk in that bag?!" Fedora Boy yelped,
scooting back on his butt to cower beneath the sinks. All the
other bystanders did likewise, flattening themselves against
the bathroom walls.

Cheri didn't so much as bat a lash while she considered
her cards. "Yes, I have a skunk," she admitted in a calm,
almost condescending voice. "A very sweet one, actually.
I hate to break it to everybody, but it doesn't exactly
smell like a bed of roses in here as it is."

She looked up from her hand and locked eyes with
Opaline. The sun had dropped lower since the game had
begun, and in the shadows Cher could see tiny bolts of
electricity spitting off Opal's shoulders.

"Cher," Iris whispered from behind her. "You don't have

to do this. We don't care about winning the collar or losing the lollipops. It's just a stupid game."

Cheri didn't care about the collar, either. Pretty as it was, she couldn't imagine ever wearing it, knowing it had been Opaline's. K-Liz must have had a strong hand of cards if Opal was willing to bet it. But after the way Opal had attacked Scarlet onstage, Cher couldn't help wanting to give her a taste of her own medicine. And for once, Cher felt confident the odds *were* in her favor. If she drew the jack of hearts, she'd have a straight flush. The most beautiful flush that bathroom had ever seen! By her superbrain estimations, she had a one-in-seventy-two-thousand-one-hundred-ninety-three chance to do so. But any other heart card would give her a good hand, and the probability of that was much higher. Even if she didn't draw a heart card at all, she could still try to bluff ol' Lizardina into folding first. Yes, it was a risk. But a calculated one.

Cheri turned her now neon-green gaze to Darth's cute face, poking out of the tote bag once more. She'd loved him since the day she first met him, four years ago in the FLab. She'd never give him up for anything in the world. And she shuddered to think why Opaline wanted him so much all of a sudden. But how sweet would it be to best Opal after she'd tried to sabotage Scarlet's audition? After she'd started the prune-juice rumor about Iris? After she'd uninvited them to her birthday party?!

Well, Cheri asked Darth, *what do you think?*

Darth's little black nose quivered as he told her, *U can betz on me.*

"C'mon," the fedora-wearing dealer urged from his hiding spot under the sinks. He reached out and lifted Mr. Grates's wristwatch from the loot pile. "We gotta wrap this game," he said, checking the time. "The night custodian will start making the rounds soon. You still in, doll-face?"

Cheri stared up at Opaline again and said with a calmness that was almost chilling, "Bet your bottom dollar I am."

Reminded of her botched audition, BellaBritney mumbled, "Gimme a wah."

"LOL, Cher," Opal grumbled, tossing her collar into the circle.

As all the onlookers recoiled into the corners of the bathroom, Darth trotted out of Cheri's tote bag and sat on top of the booty, his purple-striped tail flapping like a flag.

K-Liz drew another card. The forked end of her tongue flicked between her teeth. Her speckled snake eyes were impossible to read.

Cheri removed the one card that still didn't fit her flush and placed it facedown to the side (like a professional poker shark would). She pulled a fresh card from the deck. Her heart was pounding. What would it be?

She made a quick wish, bowed her head to hide behind her pink-tinged hair, and dared to look.

It wasn't the jack of hearts.

It wasn't the anything of hearts.

It had been a day of faces. Ick-face. Poker face. The face of the queen of hearts, staring back at Cheri since the very beginning of the game. But now Cheri allowed her face to smile.

To grin, in fact.

To grin like the goofy joker on the card she'd drawn.

Because jokers were wild. They could be whatever card she decided. Including the jack of hearts she needed to complete a straight flush.

"Call your bluff," she said to K-Liz, whose scaly forehead shot up in surprise.

"Call it!" the dealer demanded, checking the wristwatch again.

With a sour hiss, K-Liz showed her hand. Three of a kind. Not bad. But nowhere near as good as Cheri's. She laid out her cards.

"A straight flush!" Fedora Boy let out a low whistle, forgetting for a moment his fear of skunks. Then Darth squeaked happily, causing everyone to cover their heads in alarm. But the skunk just skittered down the mountain of loot and helped brush it toward Cheri with his tail.

"Oh *hello*, kitty," she purred, sweeping the big bling ring and everything else into her tote bag.

Opal jumped down from the windowsill, then swung her arm in a circle with two furious snaps. K-Liz scrambled to her feet and trailed behind BellaBritney to the bathroom door.

"Merci beaucoup, Opal," Cheri called over her shoulder as all the other students filed out. "Your black pearls are going to look super-pretty on Skeletony."

"But here," Scarlet said, untying the bow on her own plain paper collar as Opal passed by. "Your neck must feel naked now, so why don't you take mine?"

"Ooh!" Opal fumed, snatching the cutout coffee filter from Scarlet's hand and crumpling it in her fist. As she stomped out the door, a trace of brussels sprout sweat socks fading in her wake, the sound of thunder bounced around the empty boys' room.

Or was it empty?

Mr. Grates was gone. Fedora Boy was gone. O+2 had left in defeat. All the onlookers had exited. But . . .

"What's that red fuzz sticking up above the toilet stall?" Iris wondered.

"Why are two doors still closed?" Cheri asked, standing up.

The Ultra Violets exchanged glances. Then, without another word, Scarlet—who had been struggling to stay still through the entire poker game—ninja-kicked them open, *blam, blam!*

And there, feet balanced on the toilet seats, hands pressed against the walls of the stalls, in their black suits and sunglasses, stood Big Red and Lil' Freckles.

Aka the Black Swans.

Boys and Swirls

"'SUP, GIRLS?" BIG RED SAID WITH A SMIRK. "WHAT a coincidence, running into you three again. And your weaponized skunk. Nice skunky-skunky," he called to Darth.

Darth just swished his tail, indifferent.

"Coincidence, huh?" Iris said, ignoring the "weaponized" part of Big Red's taunts. "Gee whiz, who knew you could go bird-watching *in a bathroom!*"

"Who. Said anything. About bird-watching?" Lil' Freckles replied tersely, mucho peeved to have been caught spying for the third time. (Since the whole point of spying was to *not* get caught.) "In case you couldn't decipher. The pictograph on the door. This bathroom. Is supposed to be. For boys only!"

Iris scoffed. She was an artist. Of course she could decipher a pictograph!

"Watch them a sec," she said to Scarlet and Cheri. The mention of the pictograph had reminded her that the custodian might come around any minute now. She went to block the exit.

While Iris dragged the trash can across the tiles behind her, Scarlet stared at the Black Swans, dumbfounded. Had they really been hiding in the stalls for the whole poker game? Had they heard Opaline mocking her about the collar?

The thought of it bugged Scarlet so much, she *jetéed* up, snatched the shades from Big Red's face in mid-jump, backflipped over the stall wall, and grabbed the sunglasses off Lil' Freckles on the way down.

Both pairs of glasses splintered like dry spaghetti in her grip. This time, she didn't even bother saying sorry.

"Impressive jump, Miss Jones," Lil' Freckles stated through gritted teeth. With his sunglasses off, Scarlet could see that his eyes were navy blue. "Possibly even *superhuman*."

Cheri shot Scarlet the no-one-must-know warning look.

"Superhuman?" Scarlet repeated with a toss of her

ponytail. "What are you, some kind of comics geek? It's called gymnastics!"

"Little Orphan Annie was a comic strip," he said. "Before she became a musical."

So he *had* heard! Scarlet could feel herself starting to blush again. To stop it, she smacked herself in the arm again. At the sight of her crazy behavior, Big Red lost his smirk, shrieking like an elephant frightened of a mouse.

"*Dude*," he whispered over the wall of the stall to his partner-in-spy, "*the one in the tutu is trouble!*"

Trash can planted in front of the door, Iris joined Cher and Scar again, and the three Ultra Violets faced the two Black Swans standing on the toilets. Big Red had begun to jitter and jerk in place. Lil' Freckles held steady.

"You boys must have a serious case of pins and needles," Iris concluded, "if you've been stuck on those toilets all this time." She began to power up just a bit. Not so much that the boys would notice she was glowing. Just enough to turn up the heat in the room. Then she switched her smartphone to digi-video mode and began recording the interrogation. *Spying on the spies!* she thought. *Now's our chance to break them.*

Big Red ran a damp hand through his crinkled carrot hair, tugging it straight up till his head looked like one of those triangular rubber eraser tops you put on the ends of pencils. He jiggled a bit more above the toilet seat.

"Careful," Cheri teased, smoothing Darth's fur with her fingers. "You wouldn't want to slip and step in the toilet now, would you?"

After another twist, this one the most spastastic so far, he said, "Yeah, well, remember last time?" He grunted a little before squeezing out the next sentence. "When you said that boys come and go?"

"Yes . . . ?" Cheri said hesitantly, holding Darth closer. She wasn't sure where this was coming from. Or if she liked where it was going.

"I've really got to," he panted.

"Got to what?" Iris asked from behind the lens, zooming in on his huffing face.

"Go!" Big Red burst out. "To the bathroom!"

"Eww!" all three girls cried out together, ick-facing all over the place. Lil' Freckles covered his eyes and shook his head in shame, same as last time, except not upside down. "Agent Bristow!" he barked, and his voice boomed off the tiled bathroom walls. "I told you! Not to! Drink the sixty-four-ounce soda! Before a mission!"

"I was thirsty!" Big Red snapped. "So sue me, dude. My contract doesn't say no soda on the job. And I didn't know we'd be standing on toilets for an hour!" After this angry outburst, he crossed one leg over the other. Balancing on one foot, he bobbed in place.

The sight of the chubby, red-faced spy squatting above a toilet, dying to use it, kind of grossed Iris out. *But a documentary film director would push past the ew to the truth!* she told herself just as her phone buzzed to alert her she'd received a text. It was from Candace. Iris swiftly scanned the message. Then she focused her camera again and continued her interrogation.

"Let's get to the bottom of this," she said, slipping the latest intel into her speech. "You, Agent Sidney Bristow, allergic to peanuts, soprano soloist in your kindergarten glee club, could wet your pants any minute now."

Big Red's eyes popped wide open at the sound of his full name and those private biographical details. He scowled at the camera, sweat beading across his upper lip.

"Which means you, Agent Jack Baxter"—

Iris turned her lens on the short spy—"former peewee football wide receiver and winner of the Sync City Ironboy Triathlon for three years straight, are caught between a skunk and stinky place."

Lil' Freckles folded his arms, furious.

"Tell us what we want to know," Iris commanded, "and we'll let you go. To the bathroom."

"NEVER!" Lil' Freckles bellowed at the exact same instant Big Red blurted, "OKAY!"

Iris turned to the Ultra Violets, wrapping a long lavender strand around one finger. "Looks like we've got ourselves a standoff, girls," she said. "Any suggestions for how to break it, Scarlet? Anything that might be, ahem, 'in your file'?"

Scarlet marched back and forth in front of the two stalls like an army general, punching a fist into her open palm. Every few paces, she switched to grapevine steps—she couldn't help it. "The big one, Red, is done for," she decided. "Any second now he's going to burst."

Iris and Cheri both took a step back as Scarlet went on with her strategy.

"It's Lil' Freckles who needs to crack!" she shouted, slamming both hands against the sides of his toilet stall so hard that some of the screws popped out. "He's the one with the secrets! And I know how to get him to spill."

The smaller Black Swan went so white, even his freckles disappeared. "You wouldn't," he snarled.

"Desperate times call for desperate measures," Scarlet snarled right back.

Suddenly a staring contest was so on! Scarlet's steel-gray eyes bore through his dark blue ones until, overpowered by the sharp pong of the urinal cakes in the steamy bathroom, he blinked first.

"Last chance," Iris offered from behind her camera lens. "Tell us who you work for and what you want, or—"

"Or we'll give you a swirlie you'll never forget!" Scarlet threatened.

Big Red let out a shrill yip. A wedgie was bad. A pantsing was worse. But a swirlie?! The thought of having his head dunked in a flushing toilet made him dizzy with fear. And by a girl? Thank goodness he had already cracked.

Now if only he could pee.

"You're bluffing," Lil' Freckles uttered. His voice was so strained it sounded like he was chewing leather bubblegum.

"Who, us—bluff?" Cheri winked one bright green eye at the Black Swans as she waved her tote bag full of poker winnings in front of them.

In frustration, Lil' Freckles spit into the toilet bowl between his feet. He thumped his hands against the walls of the toilet stall, which wavered dangerously now that Scarlet had loosened the screws. He raised his head to the ceiling and growled like a trapped animal, "*Grrrrragh!*" Or maybe it was more like, *"Nnnnrruh!"* No, no, it was definitely, *"Grrrrragh!"*

And then he gave in.

"You promise you'll let my partner pee?"

"Oh man, I have got to pee *so bad*!" Big Red griped from the next-door stall.

"Promise," all three Ultra Violets said, wrinkling their noses together again. Then Iris tried to urge on Agent Baxter's confession. "We already know you work for BeauTek," she really did bluff—because they didn't actually know, they just suspected it. "We don't know why, because you seem like okay boys."

"When you're not *spying* on us!" Scarlet said. Then she spat on the floor, too, just to show she could.

"It's the Anti Clause," Lil' Freckles muttered. In the neighboring stall, Big Red was now doing a jig on the toilet seat.

"What's that?" Iris pressed. "What's the Anti Clause?"

The broken spy hung his salt-and-peppered head as he spoke, and his shoulders sagged in his black suit jacket. "It's a clause in the BeauTek contract that says anyone who's against—who's anti—BeauTek has to be stopped. By any means necessary."

"I knew it!" Scarlet shoved up her sleeves, prepared to give Lil' Freckles a swirlie anyway.

"Scarlet, no!" Iris stopped her. "Not yet! If we sink to their level, the enemy wins!"

Scarlet pirouetted and punched the towel dispenser

instead, knocking it off the wall. Through the lens of her camera phone, Iris thought she detected a frisson of fear from the tough lil' agent.

"Who believes in the Anti Clause?" she questioned him. "Whose idea was it?"

"Develon Louder's," he admitted. "President of BeauTek. But we got our orders to investigate you from her second banana, the scientist who writes all the contracts. A Dr. Trudeau."

Opaline's mom! All three Ultra Violets thought the same thing.

"But why?" Cheri asked. "Why are you spying on us?" First she'd been uninvited to Opal's birthday party. Now Opal's mother had put her on some blacklist! Her popularity was definitely taking a hit this year, and it really hurt her feelings.

Jack Baxter raised his head. He looked from Iris Tyler, holding the camera steady in front of her wild purple hair, to Cheri Henderson, cradling her pet skunk like a beauty queen's bouquet, lip quivering as if she might cry, to Scarlet Jones, who blew her long black bangs out her eyes with an angry huff. He stared longest and hardest at her, searching for any sign of weakness. And not finding a single one.

"You three are the prime suspects in the destruction of the Vi-Shush lab," he answered at last. "And the demolition of a bunch of mutant prototypes that were in development for . . . I'm not sure what. That part was blacked out of the documents."

"Confidential!" Big Red heaved.

The three girls didn't say a word. Because of course it was true. They *had* wrecked the Vi-Shush, the evil laboratory they'd stumbled upon in the Mall of No Returns when they'd sneaked away from the school trip to follow Opaline up the escalators to level C. That was when they freed Darth and all the other test animals. And took out Opal's mutant army with an ultraviolet combo of barrel turns, burning light beams, and toxic skunk stank on platform roller skates. And they'd do it all again in a heartbeat if they had to. But they couldn't tell that to the Black Swans!

Then each girl remembered Candace's advice at the diner:

Admit nothing: "We have *zero* idea what you're talking about," Iris said.

Deny everything: "As if three girls could destroy an entire lab all by themselves!" Scarlet said.

Make counteraccusations: "Maybe *you're* the ones who destroyed it," Cheri said, "and you're just looking for an escaped goat to blame! Or whatever that saying is!"

"Are you done yet?" Big Red shouted, doubled over.

"Hold it!" Iris ordered.

"I can't!" Big Red groaned.

"Last question!" Iris said, her focus back on Freckles. "What's in it for you?"

"No!" The stubborn spy clenched his jaw, turning his face away. "I can't!"

"Suit yourself," Iris said, motioning to Scarlet. "Let's give this boy a swirl."

"All right!" At the sight of Scarlet knotting up her ponytail, Jack Baxter caved completely. "It's height! Height, okay?"

"The overdue spurt," Iris breathed. "At the Tall-a-Boy Workshop, I bet!"

"You mean BeauTek promised to make you tall?" Scarlet whispered, feeling something like sympathy.

"And me thin!" Big Red added, fumbling with his belt buckle. "They said they'd get rid of my baby fat. It just might take a few years."

Right then the door banged against the trash can. The three girls ran to press against it.

"Somebody in there?" the custodian asked from out in the corridor.

"Almost done!" Iris said, dropping her voice to sound like a boy. "Darn bran muffin!"

Cheri began to giggle. She buried her face in Darth's fur to muffle the noise. The little skunk giggled, too.

"Hurry up, then," the custodian said on the other side of the door. "I'll be back."

The girls listened as he wheeled his cleaning cart away. A breeze on the backs of their necks made them spin around. The window was open.

Agent Jack "Lil' Freckles" Baxter was gone.

Agent Sidney "Big Red" Bristow had slammed the door closed to his toilet stall again.

And—ick-face alert!—*you* won't be relieved to know what he was doing. But gee whiz, he was!

15

Sprinkled and Shushed

THAT'S QUITE ENOUGH BATHROOM HUMOR FOR THIS book, readers. Number one (*tee-hee*), it's terribly immature. And number two (*tee-hoo*), like bran muffins, it's best in small doses. Taken with a spoonful of sugar. (*Mary Poppins added that last part. Girlfriend and her umbrella get around.*)

In the grand smorgasbord that is life—or, more befittingly, in the humble buffet that was the Chronic Prep cafeteria for breakfast—Opaline Trudeau had wisely avoided the bran muffins. And yet still she had an upset stomach. She had sidestepped the lemon-lime fruit cup. And yet still she had a sour frown on her face. She had politely declined the pickle omelet. Yet still her head felt scrambled. She had . . . well, you get the idea!

Opaline Trudeau was in a bad mood.

Her mother had to be at work early—as usual. Big goings-on at BeauTek: regenerating the mutant army; reinforcing the olfactory factory assembly line; and, of course, revamping the damaged Vi-Shush. So Dr. Trudeau had dropped off her daughter at school well before the bell. Hardly anyone was at Chronic Prep at that unhappy hour. Oh, the principal, Dingelmon, was probably in his office, practicing his scales before his morning announcements. And the teachers were probably in their lounge, fueling up on coffee before their first classes. And the lunch ladies were definitely in the kitchen, whipping up such gourmet delights as the aforementioned to-be-avoided-at-all-costs pickle omelet. But Opaline sat in the cafeteria alone, scraping the rainbow sprinkles off a chocolate-covered donut.

One might ask: Why get the rainbow sprinkles only to pick them off?

But you see, for Opaline, picking off the rainbow sprinkles was the best part.

It had been a blah couple of days for Opal. Her birthday party was coming up soon, so she should have been more excited. Her signature scent had been right on the nose so far—bumming out every classmate who came into contact with it. She smirked at the memory of Martin Gibbs stomping out of the boys' room like her own private Frankenstein. Of course, the über-vibrant Ultra Violets had proved cheerfully immune to her depressing perfume. BeauTek had expected that—no way could a chemical concentrate of brussels sprouts and sweat socks overpower sunshine and ballet. It irked Opal nonetheless. But her rival supergroup, O+2, was coming together, sort of. Though it had its share of problems, too. BellaBritney was constantly fighting with herself. And K-Liz had the vomitous habit of snacking on fly strips.

Then there were the auditions for the school play. Opal hadn't actually thought BellaBritney, with her split personality, stood a chance. Little Orphan Annie was neither a cheer-leader nor a beatnik. But seeing Scarlet Jones up on stage! Scarlet, who'd always been such a tomboy, singing and dancing her heart out! For a moment it reminded Opal of their childhood talent shows. For a moment, if she were to be completely deep-down honest with herself, Opal missed Scarlet. Which made her sad which made her mad which made her shoot out all the stage lights with thunderbolts.

And to pour salt on the wound, Cheri Henderson, former ditz, had won her favorite pearl collar in a card game! Opal wasn't sure how, but Cheri must have used her superpowers to do it—she saw her hair glowing magenta pink in that boys' room. It vexed Opal to no end to know that little skunk Darth was still out there, a furry olfactory factory himself! But if Opal were to be completely deep-down honest a second time, if she had Cheri's megamind, she'd use it to win at poker, too.

Because all's fair in love and war, Opal thought.

She pictured her black pearl collar on the FLab's old lab skeleton, Skeletony, wherever it was the Ultra Violets kept him now. In a bittersweet way, it gave Opal cold comfort. Cold comfort to know there was still a small part of her with the other three girls. Her ex-BFFs.

Opaline sat in the cafeteria early that morning, mulling over all this. The more she brooded, the darker the storm cloud grew above her head. When she'd finally finished scraping all the rainbow sprinkles off her donut—*Take that, Iris Tyler!*—she took a bite.

The dough part was stale.

But the chocolate icing tasted divine.

She was just swallowing her second mouthful of donut when she saw him. Albert Feinstein. Holding out his breakfast tray at the humble buffet. The open cuffs of his oversized shirt hung like blue plaid flags from his wrists. He chucked his chin at her as a wordless way of saying hello, then began to walk toward her table.

He looked decent.

He almost always did now, ever since Cheri had given him a stealth makeover. His sandy hair stuck out behind his ears, but in a cute way. He stumbled over the laces of his too-big basketball sneakers and nearly spilled his bowl of cereal, but that was cute, too. *Sugarsticks*, Opal thought grudgingly. The sight of him still scattered her storm cloud.

"Good morning, Opaline," Albert said, pulling out a chair and sitting down. Without even asking!

Still a nerd, Opal noted, with a mix of disdain and admiration. *"Good morning"? Please.*

Albert sniffed, his sinuses filling with the fetid stench of Opal's perfume. As if he could read her mind, his face began to go a bit red. But no, Opal realized, he wasn't embarrassed for his geeky greeting. He was embarrassed for *her*. "You, ah, you have some . . ." he stammered, pointing to the ring of chocolate frosting around her mouth.

Opal stared at him, raising her eyebrows in faked confusion. She could sense her storm cloud returning with a vengeance. She wondered if she should prolong the supreme awkwardness of the moment. If she should wait to make him say it. *Say it, Albert!* she dared him in her thoughts. *Say that I've got chocolate on my face—say it to my face!* But he was turning redder by the second and taking too long to spit it out. The perfume was probably having its pestiferous effect, too.

Opal lost her patience.

To Albert's complete and total shock, she grabbed his hand. With a jolt, he shot up straight in his seat: He could *feel* the sparks between them! She raised his arm off the table, and . . .

Ran the wide sleeve of his flannel shirt across her mouth. To wipe off the chocolate.

Then she dropped his hand, and it landed on the table with a *thud*.

Or was that the *thud* of Albert's pounding heart? Opaline's gesture was so surprising, even a bit savage, that it left him dumbstruck. Stunned.

"Thanks," Opal said, smiling at him sweetly. Her warm brown eyes misted over with spots of white. "Don't you just hate when that happens?"

Albert looked away, flustered. And noticed the plate with the scraped-off sprinkles. "Mmm!" he said, licking a fingertip. "Rainbow-flavored!" And he stuck his finger down to pick some up.

Opal struggled to keep her smile sweet. An idea was forming in her mind.

For the perfume rollout, she still needed a logistics

person. Someone to update the spreadsheets and monitor the stock and oversee the product distribution. BellaBritney could barely count past eight. Even when she did, she shouted, introducing each number with a "*Gimme a . . . !*"

That got old fast.

As for K-Liz, Opal had administered the official BeauTek personality analysis—drafted by her mother, naturally. She'd told clueless Karyn it was one of those trivial online friendship quizzes that girls were always taking. The results of her profile confirmed Opal's gut instincts: K-Liz would be better suited as a middle manager of the mutants.

Maybe I can't have Cher and her superbrain, Opal mused, recalling the way Cheri had freaked out about the Vi-Shush the other evening. *And Albert Feinstein is no Ultra Violet. He is, however, captain of the mathletes . . .*

As Albert sucked rainbow sprinkles off his sticky fingers, Opaline glanced around the cafeteria. She could hear the cafeteria ladies chatting and clanging pots and pans back in the kitchen. But no one else was there: no other students, no teacher on duty.

Just her and Albert.

He was prattling on about something unimportant, like the math test later that morning. Or was it the chess date he still wanted to go on? Whatever! He sounded nervous, which was good.

Opal needed him to be nervous. She needed that

nervous energy. It fed her more than any humble breakfast buffet ever could.

She leaned across the table, pretending to be interested.

Albert worked up the courage to look back again. That was his *second* mistake. Because the same faint, foul smell from before suddenly made him feel quite queasy. And Opaline's eyes seemed to be spiraling like pinwheels, warm chocolate brown spun through with sugary white injected with eerie pale orange that crackled like . . .

"Oh, Albert," Opal imitated, teasing him in a singsong tone as he began to sway back and forth in his seat. "You, ah, you have . . ." *She* wasn't afraid to say it straight to his face! "You have a sprinkle on your mouth." As she looked closer, all the amusement left her voice. "A purple one," she added flatly. (*That* was his *first* mistake!)

"I do?" Albert asked. But before he could say another word, Opaline licked her own pinkie finger, reached across the table, and placed it on the purple sprinkle. On his lips.

"Shush," she whispered, eyes spinning. And the electricity shot through her pinkie finger. To Albert's puckered lips, outlined like a neon sign. To his golden-grill braces. And on through his entire

nervous system, traveling all the way up to his brain. Where some corner of his mind, the corner of self-control, short-circuited.

Opal heard the *zzt!* of the burnout. She breathed in the wisp of smoke wafting from his ears.

"Shushed," Albert droned back. "I am completely and totally shushed."

With her free hand, Opal swung a wide circle.

"*O na na,*" she sang softly to herself. And she snapped her fingers up high. "*What's my name?*" And she snapped her fingers down low.

And finally she brushed the offending purple sprinkle away.

When Albert Feinstein slumped back in his chair, his mind was no longer his own. He may as well have been a zombie. Okay, not a zombie, because zombies are gross and dead and decaying and stuff. But a slave to Opaline. A zombo.

And the substitute math brain she needed.

16

Fifty Shades of Purple

STAY CALM. *DARK LAVENDER LACE* DEEP BREATHS.
lilac zebra stripes *I have not rainbowed.* *periwinkle paisleys* *I am not going to rainbow.* *indigo camouflage* *There will be no rainbowing.* *burgundy strawberries* *We're just hanging out.* *hot pink polka dots* *He is cute, though.* *crimson hearts* *And kind.* *fuchsia smiley faces* *But no one must know.* *plum exclamation points* *No one must know!*

Five minutes before, Iris had excused herself from the small table in the quaint storefront café of Gelato Be Chilling Me. Now she was hiding in the bathroom, her face flashing through fifty shades of purple in fifty different patterns as she tried to burn off some of the ultraviolet energy that was threatening to bust out of her. She stared at herself in the mirror, blinking like a holiday display. She gave herself her sternest no-one-must-know warning glance.

Because even though they *were* just hanging out, depending on how you wanted to *define* hanging out, Iris was (OMV!) on her first date with Sebastian. Who was sitting out at their table, probably wondering what had happened to her.

When Sebastian called and asked her to meet up, Iris had rainbowed insanely, all over the place. But luckily, at the time, she was high up in Club Very UV. Sebastian couldn't see her. (They weren't on video chat: He'd made an old-school phone call, which Iris found totes charming.) And as far as the rest of Sync City could tell, it was just a beautiful natural sight. People thought rainbows were beaming down on the buildings. Not shooting up from one of them.

That afternoon, once Iris had finally powered down, she had a heartfelt convo with Cheri and Scarlet. She worried whether it was fair of her to go out with Sebastian when she knew she could never ever be completely honest with him. She could never ever tell him her secret identity as a superhero.

"It's just one date," Cheri had said with a flip of her berry-red waves. "Don't overthink it!" Of course, as she was saying it, Cheri was already overthinking it big-time, running a complicated spreadsheet in her mind about all the possible things that could go wrong on the date, and how Iris should deal if they did.

"Every time you feel like you might start rainbowing or glowing ultraviolet," Scarlet had said while crossing the floor of the clubhouse in *chaîné* turns, "just give yourself a thump in the arm! That always helps me."

Iris didn't follow that advice exactly—it sounded too painful! But she did quit lollipops cold turkey two days before, so that she wouldn't be too hyped up on candy. And she searched online for meditation tips. It said that whenever she felt her thoughts wandering—or, in her case, her temperature rising—she should focus on her breathing and repeat her mantra.

"*OhmV*," she repeated softly in the restroom of the gelato shoppe.

Probably what had helped her the most, though, was something completely random that Iris remembered out of the blue from the cover of a fashion magazine. She'd seen it at the dentist's office, on the table in the waiting room. Next to the photo of a glamorous actress, a headline read: ***Want to Keep Him Interested? Keep the Mystery Alive!***

I can do that! Iris realized with relief. Maybe keeping secrets would be a good thing? If that's what it said in magazines!

Iris took one last look at herself in the mirror. Face:

pattern-free. Eyes: pale blue. Hair: wild violet. Check check check! It was as Zen as she was going to get.

Sebastian was waiting by the front door, all tall, dark, and awesome. He smiled when he saw her, and his shiny black hair fell into his eyes as usual.

"Hey," he said, flipping his hoverboard off up the floor and holding the door open. "Everything okay?"

"Viomazing," Iris murmured. She thought about coming up with more of an explanation, but she remembered again about keeping the mystery alive. So she just smiled back. "Thanks again for the ice cream."

As she said it, though, something caught her eye.

Something past Sebastian, way in the back of the shoppe.

Gelato be kidding me, she thought. *Not now!*

Time froze like ice cream as Iris quickly took in the scene. By the counter, a bearded man in a motorcycle jacket was leaning over a little boy, who was bawling his eyes out. At first Iris thought the man was trying to steal the boy's double-dip waffle cone. But as he crouched closer, a snout of matted gray-brown fur came into focus. And bristly twitching whiskers. And four long incisor teeth that looked sharp enough to gnaw through . . .

The boy let out another fearful sob.

A mutant! Iris could feel her ultraviolet rising. And now it had absolutely nada to do with Sebastian. Time started melting again as Iris met his eyes. She had to think fast. Of all the scenarios on Cheri's first-date spreadsheet, "encounter with a biker rat" was not one of them!

"Oopsie," Iris said with a shrug. "I forgot my rhinestone stylus in the restroom."

"Your rhinestone stylus?" Sebastian repeated befuddledingly (*not a real word, but a good one*). "But why were you using it in—"

"Meet me outside, okay?" Iris cut him off with her sparkliest smile. "Back in a flash!" And then, because she didn't know what else to do, and the seconds on the symbolic ice-cream clock were dripping away, and a giant mutant biker rat in the back of the gelato shoppe was about to have two scoops of little boy with a cherry on top, because of *all that*, Iris stretched up her hand and . . . tousled Sebastian's shaggy hair? Before spinning him around by the shoulders and giving him a gentle shove down the steps.

"What'd you do that for?" Sebastian laughed, stumbling out into the sunshine. The sun felt warm on his face. But not nearly as hot as Iris's hand had felt in his hair. Every time he started to think she was quite a serious girl, she'd do something kooky. Like graffiti a wolfman on the monorail wall, or paint a flower instead of saying her name. Which was all very strange. And super-intriguing. She was like a riddle wrapped in a mystery tied up with curly purple ribbons, that Iris. Sebastian stood on the sidewalk in a bit of a purple haze, pushing back his hair and trying to get his head straight.

On the corner across the street, a clown with a bunch of heart-shaped balloons for sale was blowing a fierce saxophone solo.

Sebastian may have been lost in his thoughts, with the saxophone serenade of a street clown as his soundtrack. But Iris was already in the back of the shoppe.

She lowered her eyes, which by now were blazing the whitest ultraviolet. She inched along the counter, getting as close as she could to the nasty biker rat. She was radiating so much heat that all the gelato turned to sugary soup in the containers behind the counter, but that couldn't be helped. With a hair-thin beam from her pinkie finger, she speed-painted the dollop of melting ice cream on the crying boy's cone into the hissing face of a tomcat.

"Eeek!" the ratman squeaked, skittering back a step. The boy dropped his weird feline ice cream and ran off to find his mommy.

Iris aimed her scalding-hot ultraviolet eyebeams at the ratman's kneecaps. His jeans burned through to holes in an instant, and his skin started to sizzle. With a shriek he tumbled to all fours and scurried out the back door. Just as a waiter, way too late, went running behind him with a broom. And slipped in the ice-cream mess the little boy had made.

Gelato be spilling he? Iris thought, and tried not to giggle. Under the circumstances!

Sensing that her eyes were still beyond the pale, Iris kept her head down. She hid her glowing hands in her pockets as she stepped around the puddle of waiter and went out the back, too. The charred ratman was just peeling out of the parking lot on his rumbling motorcycle. To what sounded like the wail of a fierce saxophone solo? How odd. But Iris didn't chase the mutant. She just took a moment to "*OhmV*" and to power down again.

When her eyes no longer burned, Iris glanced around the parking lot. Sebastian's name was still spray-painted on the dumpster, her purple namesake blossom beside it. That made her smile.

She walked around the side of the building to meet Sebastian out front. He was balancing atop his hoverboard, searching for her.

"Hey!" he said as she approached. "Did you see it?"

"See what?" Iris asked, linking her arm through his and steering him away from the café.

"All these people came running out of the ice cream place, screaming about a giant rat!"

"Ew, really?" Iris said, trying to sound surprised. And feeling a bit bad that she was lying. "No way! How gross!"

"But at least you got your stylus, right?" Sebastian nudged his shoulder against hers as he said it, trying to read the expression on her face. But it was hidden behind all her purple curls.

"My stylus?" Iris said, then remembered. "Oh, my rhinestone stylus!" She patted her messenger bag. "Yup, it's back where it belongs."

As they continued walking along to the wild howl of the clown's saxophone, it occurred to Iris that keeping the mystery alive was going to be exhausting. Hopefully worth it. But exhausting!

16¼*

Black Balloon
{*Because Iris's Date Shouldn't Have Ended Like This}

EXCEPT FOR THAT PART WITH THE MUTANT RAT AND THE melting ice cream, it was a great date. Iris kept her rainbowing under control without ever having to smack herself in the arm. And she handled a mini-crisis that even Cheri's graph hadn't predicted!

Iris and Sebastian had spent the rest of the afternoon wandering around the Kitchen Sync neighborhood. They talked about the good and the bad of graffiti. About what role an artist should fill in society. Sebastian let her try out his hoverboard, holding her hands to help her keep her balance.

He let her try on his tattered steampunk top hat, too. And he bought her a blue heart-shaped balloon as a souvenir— when the street-corner clown finally finished his raging sax solo!

Sebastian had offered to walk Iris all the way back to her apartment building, but she'd politely declined. She told him she was supposed to meet Cheri and Scarlet in Chrysalis Park, which she wasn't. The truth was, Iris just wanted some alone time, to mull over the date and maybe sketch a few impressions on her iCanvas. Since she didn't want Sebastian to think she was blowing him off, she fibbed a little. A little more than she already had that day. And she worried again if "keeping the mystery alive" was really just a clever way of saying "be a pretty little liar."

Iris shook out her curls. "No one must know," she said into the wind as she leaned against the latticed Plexiglas fence that bordered the orange brick path of the park. With the string of her heart-shaped balloon wrapped around her wrist, she fished in her messenger bag for a lollipop. Blueberry, her favorite.

It tasted so sweet. And the Joan River looked so lovely at dusk, the sea creatures flashing their primary colors beneath the water's surface, the frothy caps of the deep green currents kissed with sunset tangerine. Suddenly Iris was overwhelmed with wonder at the magic of everything. Of ice cream melting in a bowl, of the endless patterns of purple in the world, of Sebastian's tapered fingers holding her on the hoverboard, even of the clown's saxophone symphony! It was all so strange and beautiful, Iris thought she might cry. Her heart swelled, and she imagined it soaring as high as the blue balloon in the river breeze, and she wanted to send out a triple rainbow like a love letter in the sky to all of Sync City, her home.

But she reminded herself she wasn't supposed to do that. That there had been way more than the average number of rainbows lately as it was!

Instead, Iris closed her eyes for a second or three and twirled her pinkie finger around one of her purple ringlets. When she opened her eyes again, the orange brick path was cheerful yellow.

She began skipping, she began spinning, she began *easing* on down the bricks, her blue heart-shaped balloon floating above her head.

But as she neared the park gates, the silhouette of a familiar figure slowed her in her tracks. Yes, Iris could tell as she stepped closer; it was definitely her. Arms folded. Hair pulled back tight in barrettes. Peter Pan collar.

"Hello, Iris," Opaline said coldly.

Iris was in such a buoyant mood, she took a crazy chance. She threw her arms wide open. And she wrapped Opal up in a big bear hug. Like nothing had ever gone wrong between them.

Like they were still best friends.

"Hi, Opaline!" Iris whispered, right in her ear. "I miss you."

It's hard to describe what happened next. Here goes:

Opal began to melt. Not like the Wicked Witch of the West in *The Wizard of Oz*, even though she was standing on a yellow brick road. Not even like the ice cream at Gelato Be's café. Just on the inside, when she felt the solar warmth of Iris's embrace. She let the tough knot of anger that was always in the pit of her stomach loosen. And Iris's ultraviolet light beamed around both of them, enveloping Opal like a safe cocoon in Chrysalis Park.

But then . . .

(*Didn't you just know there was going to be a "but then"?*)

But then Opal stopped feeling and started thinking again. About O+2 and zombo Albert and her birthday party. About Cheri turning her down and stealing her pearl collar. About Scarlet dancing in the dark at the audition. And most of all about Iris. About purple sunshiny Iris, who she blamed for everything.

A storm cloud formed above the two girls. Opal clamped her hands on Iris's shoulders and concentrated all her powers on sending out wave after shockwave of electricity. Both girls' hair stood on end, Iris's doubling in length as her curls snapped straight as live wires. With the high voltage coursing through her, she quaked so hard her teeth clattered. A sudden tsunami of sorrow threatened to engulf her, and the putrid scent of Opal's strange perfume made her gag.

Iris hadn't wanted to hurt Opal. The exact opposite! But now she had no choice. She could feel every nerve in her body vibrating. If she didn't get free from Opal's electric grip, she was afraid she might have a seizure!

So Iris concentrated all of *her* powers and started burning back, blazing hotter than the sun. Passersby didn't know what was going on—night had been just about to fall, and all of a sudden they were bathed in broad daylight?

The two girls stood locked together like that, Iris convulsing with Opal's electric currents, Opal baking under Iris's ultraviolet heat, until finally the blue heart-shaped balloon burst in midair. And like an exploding atom, the two girls split apart.

Opal fell to her knees with a hideous shriek. Iris staggered back, still twitching, and erupted into tears.

"Opal," she managed to sob through rattling teeth, "what is wrong with you?" She gasped for breath. Teardrops spilled from her ultraviolet eyes, evaporating the instant they touched the hot skin of her cheeks. "I was trying to be nice!"

"That's your problem, Iris!" Opal screamed back, looking at the sore red blisters Iris had burned into the palms of her hands. "Nobody asked you to! Your niceness makes me sick!"

Iris straightened up. Trembling, she looped the trailing string of the balloon around her fingers until its burnt remains were in her fist. *My first-date souvenir from Sebastian*, she thought. *A black-and-blue heart.* As she tucked the tattered scraps into her messenger bag, her real heart ached, too.

Gone was the joy she'd felt just minutes before. She looked down the park's riverside path. *Good-bye, yellow brick road*, she thought sadly. And with a blink of her brimming eyes, she turned it orange again. Without another word, without a glance at Opaline, still on her knees, Iris walked out of the park.

And then the sky went velvet dark, as if all the stars in the galaxy had burned out along with one bruised balloon.

Just Thinkin' About...

BUT, JUST LIKE IT SAYS IN THE SONG, THE SUN DID
come out tomorrow. The Ultra Violets didn't even have
to bet a thing: not bottom dollars or black pearl collars or
superskunks. They just had to hang on till, "come what
MAAAAAAY . . . !"

"Oh!" Curled up on the marshmallow couch in Club
Very UV, Cheri covered her ears. "Scar, you sound good, but
should you maybe save your voice?"

"OKAAAAAY!" Scarlet sang out. Then, abruptly bashful,
she flopped down from the *arabesque* pose she'd been
holding and buried her face in the silver beanbag. Breaking
news: She got the part! She was one of Chronic Prep's three
rotating Annies, and rehearsals officially began . . . the day
before tomorrow.

While Scarlet burrowed into the beanbag and Cheri
went back to her book report, Iris stared up at the sun from
the massive flower window. The sun was Iris's favorite star,

and it did make her feel energized all over again, like anything was possible. Even rescuing Opaline from the darkness.

"I cannot believe you got your hug on, right there in the park!" Cheri exclaimed, setting her book aside. Iris's story, from her date with Sebastian to the motorcycle rat of Kitchen Sync to the major power outage with Opaline, was much more interesting.

Iris smiled to herself, because she couldn't quite believe it, either. "I guess it was Operation Get-O, version two-point-no," she said, walking from the window back to the long marble table. "Plan 'Share the Love.'"

"With a megawatt psycho?" Scarlet remarked, her voice muffled by the beanbag.

"Don't call her that!" Cheri stifled her own laugh. "Opal is . . . I don't know what she is." She looked to Darth, but he just shrugged his little skunk shoulders. "Disturbed for sure."

"What was she even doing there?" Scarlet sat up, her face red from squishing it. "What if she's following us? For real, Cher, she's scary. She could have electrocuted Iris!"

"But she didn't at first," Iris said, thinking back. "For a second or three, everything was . . . was pure violet! And I truly thought . . . I don't know." She could sense Cheri's and Scarlet's doubts. But Iris was such a starry-eyed optimist, she said it out loud anyway. "I thought we were going to make up."

Scarlet groaned. Cheri was silently skeptical. At the table,

Iris traced her finger around the ruins of the blue balloon. She'd decided to add it to her scrapbook. Even though it was in tatters, there was still, she thought, something precious about it. Maybe just knowing the story behind it, her strange yesterday, was what made the balloon worth saving. Maybe that was why she still wanted to save Opal, too. On the outside, Opal seemed like a lost cause. But Iris could never forget Opal's inside story.

"I just felt so sad after, you know?" she said, her gaze drifting over to Skeletony, who was indeed wearing Opal's black pearl collar. The girls had put it there, around the bony white vertebrae, as a joke. Now it looked a bit eerie.

"Have you seen her bummed-out lunch table lately?" Scarlet said, scissor-kicking from her beanbag seat. "It's like, who died? Opal has definitely got a way of killing the mood in the cafeteria."

"Maybe everyone who sits next to her loses their appetite," Iris commented. "That perfume she keeps wearing is literally sickening. I thought I was going to barf in the park."

"Then there was that time she tried to get me to join O+2," Cheri said with a sigh as she filed her pinkie finger. "That was superdepressing."

"When did that happen?" Iris asked, as Scarlet sprang to her feet again.

Cheri ceased her filing. "Alas," she realized, two petals of pink blooming on her cheeks. "I never did tell you, did I?"

"Tell us *what*?" Scarlet demanded, dancing worrisome little *soubresaut* jumps. Iris began anxiously twisting a tendril of her hair.

Darth snuggled into Cheri's lap to give her moral support while she explained. "Scarlet, you were so nervous about your audition," she began. "And Iris, you were so hung up on Sebastian . . ."

"And?!" Iris and Scarlet said together.

"And I didn't want to upset you more!" Cheri cried. "I said no, obvi! But Opal said . . . she said she wanted my brain."

"Gah!" Scarlet covered her head with her hands as she leaped in place. Darth covered his with his paws, chittering.

"Not in the Frankenstein transplant way," Cheri said, stroking the skunk to soothe him. She wasn't quite sure why she was defending Opal, considering the girl had just shocked the hair straight on Iris. Maybe it was because Cheri still remembered Opal's inside story, too. "More like . . ." Cheri trailed off, and all three girls concentrated for a moment.

"More like in the *Feinstein* mathlete way!" Iris gasped, snapping her fingers.

"Well," Cheri huffed, buffing her nails against Darth's fur, "I actually think I'm smarter than Albert, but—"

"But she couldn't *control* you, Cher!" Scarlet said, smacking her forehead a little harder than necessary.

"And she *could* control Albert." Iris snapped her fingers again. "And K-Liz." She swung her arm up high and snapped there. "And BellaBritney." Another snap down low.

"Is that what she's doing?" Cheri wondered. "Blowing the fuses in everyone's minds? But how?"

"I'm not sure, but have you seen the way Albert's been following her around, all stumbly and blank-faced?" Iris asked.

Cheri frowned. She *had* seen it, and it *had* bugged her, but she'd told herself she was just being vain. After all, there was a time when Albert followed *her* around like a puppy dog, too. There was The Kiss That Changed Everything! And while Cheri never did think of Albert as boyfriend material, she did still have a special place in her heart for her first successful stealth makeover project.

"We've got to save Albert," she stated.

"And we've got to stop Opal from short-circuiting anyone else!" Scarlet shouted, springing so high that her ponytail almost got tangled in the holiday lights they'd strung all across the ceiling. "At least she's only zapped Albert so far," she said as she landed in *demi-pointe*. "K-Liz and BellaBrit are mutants."

Wheels spinning, Iris reeled around in the fuzzy orange egg chair. "True. But she threatened to take over the entire class. And remember how Martin Gibbs clawed at Cheri in the hallway after your audition?"

"Ruh-roh," Scarlet muttered, thinking back on it.

"Opal got an entire *crew* of mutants to obey her every command at the Vi-Shush . . ." Iris let the sentence hang.

Cheri's mind was in overdrive, too, so much so that her hair started to glow magenta right there in CVUV. "If Opal got the whole class together, like at an assembly . . ."

"Or at the school play!" Scarlet realized, horrified.

"Or," Iris said, arching an eyebrow as she looked from one Ultra Violet to the other, "at a *birthday party* . . ."

"OMV!" Cheri and Scarlet cried out together.

That had to be it: Opaline was planning a mass reprogramming at her own party!

For once Cheri was *thrilled* to be uninvited. Even if she had already planned some awesome party-crasher outfits.

Are You There, Candace?

ALL OF A SUDDEN, RIGHT THERE IN CVUV, IRIS, SCARLET, and Cheri had an overwhelming urge to write down their phone numbers and wash some cars? All three could hear the notes of a pop-music synth violin in their heads. They lined up in the middle of the clubhouse and broke into song:

> *Hey, we had a breakthrough!*
> *That plan is cray-z!*
> *We must stop Opal!*
> *Call Candace, maybe?*

Then, as if this bizarre musical interlude had never gotten hold of them, the three girls each grabbed a seat at the long marble table and video-buzzed Candace at the FLab. They leaned in close together so that she could see all three of their faces on the laptop screen.

"You took your time with the call!" Candace said. She must have just gotten her hair cut, because her bangs were so baby they were practically newborn. Weirdly, tucked behind her ears, she had not one but TWO sporks. The pointy ends stuck out like stainless steel cyber tulip clips. No, they did.

"Candace!" Iris said, surprised. "Did you accidentally pick up *another* spork from Tom's Diner?"

Candace hardly seemed to care that she was attracting sporks the way a refrigerator does magnets. "What happened with the Black Swans?" she asked. "Did they rock the pier or what?"

"Very funny, Candace," Iris said. "And thanks for your text. We totally busted those spy boys."

"Yeah!" Scarlet pushed her face in front of the laptop's camera. "At a poker game in the boys' room!" She furrowed her freckles, recalling the pugnacious agent with the salt-and-pepper hair. "But the lil' one climbed out the window."

"The big one is kind of a bully," Cheri stated with a roll of her eyes.

"They're working for BeauTek, just like we suspected! But that's not why we're calling, maybe!" Iris wedged her chin on top of Cheri's head, a few of her purple ringlets tickling Cher's nose.

"The Black Swans we can handle!" Scarlet said.

"Boys come and go," Cheri added, cheek-to-cheek with Scar.

"But—" Iris began, Scarlet shouting, "SPOILER ALERT!" so loud that it made the speaker crackle on Candace's side of the call.

"But," Iris continued, rubbing her ear, while beneath her Cheri and Scarlet bickered in low tones about whether it really *was* a spoiler, "we figured out that Opal is planning to shock our entire class!"

"INTO HER ELECTRIC ZOMBIE SLAVES!" Scarlet said, shouting again.

"At her birthday party!" Iris piped in.

"That we weren't invited to," Cheri couldn't help saying.

Then the Ultra Violets fell silent. Their stares were holding. Their breathseses (= *plural*) were holding, too.

Waiting for Candace's reply. Waiting for Candace's advice. Waiting for Candace's instructions.

Instead, she gave them nothing at all. Stood up. And went offscreen altogether.

"Hey!" Scarlet cried out. "Where d'you think you're going, lady?"

. . .

dot dot dot

DOT DOT DOT!

"Candace?" Iris spoke at last to the empty screen. "Are you there?"

"It's us," Cheri whispered.

"The Ultra Violets?" Scarlet said snarkastically.

They could hear a voice somewhere in the FLab proclaiming, "That ectoplasm isn't going to mop itself up, you know!" Then, as suddenly as she'd left, Candace returned to the screen. She bent her head in close, her supershort bangs like a dirty-blond picture frame across her forehead.

"Okay, UVs," she said quickly, glancing behind both shoulders so often that the two silver sporks flashed in front of the screen so fast that the only thing missing was a tossed salad between them. "This is the deal: To keep Opaline from reprogramming your entire grade, you have to find an antidote to her electrocute-ability."

"Which is really not very cute at all," Cheri muttered.

"But what is it?" Iris asked. "Where do we find it? How do we use it?"

"Be careful!" Candace said, answering none of those questions. "And remember, if you need any help, you've got my number. So call me, maybe. Coddington out!"

Before the girls could add any more questions to the unanswered list, Candace lowered her screen, and theirs went blank.

Mama Drama

'TWAS A CLASSIC RUSE. A WILY SUBTERFUGE. A TRIED-and-true trick.

Iris told her mother, Dr. Tyler, that she was sleeping over at Cheri's house that night.

Cheri told her mother, Dr. Henderson, that she was sleeping over at Scarlet's.

Scarlet told her mother, Dr. Jones, that she was sleeping over at Iris's.

And instead all three girls (plus one skunk) had laid low at Club Very UV until after dark. Then they changed into their catsuits—which were really just black leotards and tights, but catsuits sounds cooler. Iris wove her hair into two long braids and pinned them into purple cinnamon buns over her ears, Princess Leia–style. Cheri discovered her leotard had a cat tail sewn to the bottom, leftover from some past Halloween costume, and she decided to work it. With a black eye pencil she drew thick lines over and out from her lids. She pushed back her hair with a kitten-eared headband. And for a touch of sparkle, she slipped on the Hello Kitty bling ring she'd won in the poker game. Scarlet laced up a brand-new pair of red satin ballet slippers—which she found *terribly* pretty—to go with her red tutu.

The three girls checked one another's outfits and agreed they were purrrfectly dressed.

To break into the FLab.

To sneak out, Scarlet wanted to climb up to the clubhouse roof and then bungee down the side like Spider-Man, the same way the spy boys had the first time the girls caught them. But that plan had problems. First, they didn't have bungee cords. Second, Iris was sure the wind would ruin her hair. Third, Cheri said Darth had a slight fear of heights.

Instead, the girls simply slipped back down the spiral iron staircase, from the clubhouse into Iris's bedroom, and then out her apartment door. As they left her room, Iris quickly disguised the three of them as junk mail, patterning their leotards with home decor catalogs and supermarket flyers. Her mom always ignored the snail mail, letting it pile up until Iris recycled it. But no worries: After a long day at the FLab, Dr. Tyler was already sound asleep on the couch. From the TV, an old episode of *The Twilight Zone* cast blue-gray shadows on her face.

Downstairs in the lobby of the building, the doorman smiled when he saw them.

"Off to a party, girls?" he asked.

"Off to stop one, actually," Scarlet said, shim-sham-shimmying out onto the street, while Iris just waved good night.

"Remind me again why we couldn't ask Candace to get this stuff?" Scarlet hissed. She didn't know why she was whispering. No one else was in the Highly Questionable Tower that late at night. Whispering just felt like the clandestine thing to do. Under the circumstances.

The girls had broken into the Fascination Laboratory exactly how you'd expect them to: Iris camouflaging the three of them as they glid (*we spell it like that!*) past the security guards and shot up forty-two flights in the clear crystal elevator; Cheri using her computer brain to crack all the digital passcodes; and Scarlet giving the steel security doors a hefty *rond de jambe en l'air* roundhouse kick when they still wouldn't budge.

Now they were creeping around in the dark in their catsuits.

"She didn't offer to on video-chat," Iris hissed back. "Doesn't Candace seem extra spacey lately?"

"Maybe she's dating an astronaut!" Cheri whispered. She meant it seriously, but once she heard it out loud, she started giggling at how silly it sounded. Iris and Scarlet broke into giggles, too, the beams from their flashlights bouncing off jars and beakers as the girls shook with laughter.

The *last* time the girls were in the FLab was right after Opal went evil. While their moms were out at some snoozy afternoon symposium, Iris, Scarlet, and Cheri had met with Candace. That was when they'd vowed to do everything in their powers (both super- and non-) to turn Opal good again. Because the *second*-to-last time they were in the FLab, four years before, was when Candace had been careless and Cheri had sneezed and Iris had drop-kicked the vat of Heliotropium goo that had then splattered all over them. *Fourever* altering the four best friends blah blah blah!

Somehow, the strange purple goo that had made Iris, Scarlet, and Cheri supergirls was also the same strange purple goo that had made Opal such an electroshockingly mean one. To concoct an antidote, like Candace had mentioned, Iris had done some research. Cheri had done up a little FLaboratory shopping list. And Scarlet had done a tango.

"Being here in the dark really reminds me of that night!" Cheri said softly after the giggle fit had passed. Hiding in her tote bag, Darth squeaked—he remembered it, too.

Iris unwrapped a lollipop, the waxed paper crackling in the quiet as if she were in a movie theater and not a top-secret science lab. "It's v beautiful, isn't it?" She stopped for a moment to look out the FLab's rock-crystal windows at the skyline of Sync City, searching for the pulsing purple light atop their clubhouse.

"And double-v creepy," Scarlet added. She was peering at what might have been a baby spiderpig, or maybe a giant sea monkey, floating in the murky water of a fat mason jar.

"Well, I've got the *Hevea Brasiliensis* cells," Iris whispered, reading the label off a Petri dish, "to replicate the latex."

"And I've got the, um, conjugated hydrocarbon dienes for the polymers," Cheri checked off their list.

"And I've got the purple food coloring from home," Scarlet reminded them.

"And *we've* got *you*, naughty girls."

At the sound of the chilly, clipped voice, the Ultra Violets froze in place, and Iris's Princess Leia buns spontaneously popped loose, the two braids sprouting out like she was a purple Pippi Longstocking instead. Lights flooded the FLab, brighter than a thousand camera flashes. The girls rushed to cover their eyes.

"The mamarazzi!" Cheri moaned, squinting out between her fingers.

Next to her, Scarlet muttered, "Quoth the raven, d'oh!"

Standing before them, in three sets of pink bunny slippers, their lab coats belted over their bathrobes, were the girls' doctor-moms.

"How did you . . . ?" Iris began, though she wasn't sure she should ask.

Dr. Tyler, the mom who had spoken before flicking on the lights, didn't even bother to answer. She just pointed to the top shelf. At a panda bear plush toy. With wide, glassy eyes.

"Is that my old teddy-cam?!" Scarlet exclaimed.

"I brought it to the FLab for bonus security," Dr. Jones said, wringing her hands, "since I *thought* you had outgrown the need for a stuffed babysitter, Scarlet!"

"Apparently none of them has," Dr. Tyler stated matter-of-factly, one bunny-slippered foot tapping the floor.

"Mom," Iris began, "we were just, um, getting some supplies for a science fair project?"

"Latex and polymers?" she sniffed. "Are you competing against the kindergarten class? After four years of astronaut offspring boarding school, I expect more from you than common rubber balls, Iris Grace."

Iris flinched, her pigtails drooping down to her shoulders.

"And your father and I thought you had stopped these shenanigans," Dr. Jones chastened Scarlet. "Look at you! Your brand-new ballet slippers, already filthy!"

Scarlet hung her head and balanced perfectly still *en pointe*, which was very difficult to do. It took much more strength for Scarlet to hold that pose, and to hold her tongue, than it would have to pirouette around the FLab ten times.

"Cheri, honey, I'm not even going to ask what's going on with the catsuit," her mother sniped, sizing her up and down with a brisk zigzag of her finger. "On a school night?" She must have come straight from the bath, because Dr. Henderson's hair was up in a towel turban and her face was covered in a chalky white mask. Yet she had gone to the trouble of slicking on some red lipstick. She reminded Cheri of the Joker—from her poker cards *and* from Batman.

"Meouch, Mommy!" Cher pouted, folding her arms to hide the blingy Hello Kitty ring. "I tried not to overaccessorize!"

"Well, whatever you three were attempting to prove with this little experiment," Dr. Tyler said, eyeballing the shirking Violets, "we've got the result. And it's conclusive." As the other two mothers nodded along, she declared, "You girls are grounded."

Gossip Girls

IN THREE SEPARATE BEDROOMS ACROSS SYNC CITY, three separated supergirls sat on their beds that Friday after school. One surrounded herself with her stuffed animals and started painting her nails lilac and black. One lay on her back and walked her feet up the wall until she was in a headstand on her mattress. One paused from the portrait she was drawing to gaze out her window at the raindrops.

At the exact same moment, each girl breathed a deep sigh.

Then, her nail polish nearly dry, Cheri could bear it no longer. She picked up her phone and began passionately texting.

The insta-blurt popped up in the corner of Iris's iCanvas digital sketchpad:

chericheri: how is darth?!?

Using the tip of her rhinestone stylus, Iris tapped back a quick response:

purplegirl: safe up in club dont worry!

Cheri, who was a master at concealing clandestine pets, had discreetly handed off Darth to Iris before her Joker-faced mother had marched her back home last night. Cheri's mom had awful allergies, so Cheri had never been allowed to have even a hamster all to herself. Not that her mother would have allowed a skunk in the house, even if she wasn't allergic!

chericheri: what r u doing? im bored 😞
purplegirl: ❤drawing sebastian❤
scarlojones: how can u think abt boyz at time like this? u r obsessed!

Scarlet had joined the conversation.

NW! Iris typed back. UVs 4evs! drawing helps me think ☺ Operation Get-O Plan D?!? MUST. CRASH. PARTY!

For those keeping track, Operation Get-O Plan A was the derailed ice-cream intervention. Plan B—which wasn't really planned, it sort of just happened—was the surprise hug in Chrysalis Park. Plan C was . . . well, as a matter of fact, it *did* involve rubber, thank you very much, Iris's smartypants mom! But more on that later.

Plan D was yet to be D-termined.

> **chericheri:** r u sure u dont just wanna go 2 party bcuz graff boy might b there?
>
> **purplegirl:** haha o doesnt know him! but scar mayb tuff lil frecks there spying?!

Scarlet had been texting semi–upside down till this point, but when she read Iris's message, her feet fell toward her face and she tumbled backward off the bed. "Owie," she muttered from the carpet before typing her response.

scarlojones: SO?!!

chericheri: so i think he likes u do u like him alas?!

Just in case you'd forgotten, Cheri believed in love. In love against the odds! Be it vampire–werewolf, Olympian–couch potato, supergirl–clueless boy, or even supergirl–*spy*boy! On the road to true love, allegiance to an evil biocosmetic empire was, in Cheri's opinion, a minor speed bump.

Scarlet, however, was not so sure. Every time she caught herself thinking about the blue-eyed Agent Jack Baxter, she'd thump herself in the shoulder to stop it, then dance a waltz to distraction. But last night at the FLab, balancing there in her pointe shoes before the doctor-moms, hanging her head and holding strong to her position, she remembered him doing the same. The only reason he'd cracked on the toilet was to help his obnoxious partner, Big Red. That was honorable, wasn't it? Even if he was spying on them for BeauTek?

scarlojones: hes a bad guy u guys! end of story!

chericheri: i think hes cute. purrfkt 4 u!

purplegirl: mayb just confused like O? mayb we can turn him?

scarlojones: u cant just paint them good riri! not that e-z.

Scarlet had a point. Never mind the Black Swans: Ever

207

since Iris had been grounded, she'd been trying to think of how the UVs' superpowers could stop Opaline from zombotomizing their entire class. With her crazy electric currents, Opal could somehow short-circuit brains. How could Iris's camouflage and solar radiation, or Scarlet's dancing and strength, or Cheri's psychic computer stop that? How could they even try? The party was tomorrow and they were forbidden to leave their rooms!

Iris wrapped a pinkie finger around one of her purple tendrils, tugging on it as she thought for a second or three.

oops hear mom . . . The message came in from Cheri.

me 2 ruh-roh! Scarlet typed.

LOOK OUT! Iris insta-blurted, right before her own mother opened her bedroom door to check on her. Iris quickly clicked to some homework for her science class and flashed it at her mom as proof of her good behavior. But different scenes played out at Scarlet's and Cheri's:

Dr. Jones: "I thought I told you no Interweb!"

Scarlet: "But Mom, I was only texting!"

Dr. Henderson: "I don't care, give that to me right now. No phone for the rest of the weekend."

Cheri: "But *Mommm!*"

Doors slam, mothers exit. Scarlet punches her pillows, Cheri stamps her feet. Cheri breaks a nail. Scarlet breaks a lamp (completely by accident). Then both go to their bedroom windows...

Both go to their bedroom windows because of the last thing Iris had written:

LOOK OUT!

So they did.

And there, as if a ray of sunshine had burned through the mists, written in the thick gray rain clouds covering Sync City, was a message. Cheri and Scarlet had to read the blue-sky words fast; already the winds were blowing them to wisps:

¡have an idea!
watch this space!

Prism Break

IT WAS STILL GRAY ON SATURDAY. NOT DOWNPOURING, but threatening to, and drizzling now and then.

In the backyard of her family's bluestone townhouse, Scarlet rain-danced, pausing every so often to, as Iris had sky-written, "watch that space." She'd been making such a wretched racket bouncing off the walls in her bedroom, her mother finally had given in and told her to get out! Outside, that is. "Maybe some fresh air and exercise will calm you down," Dr. Jones had said, although she doubted it. Scarlet never stopped for long.

Scarlet was glad for a chance to stretch her legs and practice her routines for the school play. But her thoughts churned like the clouds in the sky, and no number of leaps or twirls could clear them. Soon Opaline's birthday party would be starting. By Monday morning, would she, Cheri, and Iris be the only students left in their right minds? What was Opal going to *do* with their class once they were completely under her control? And what if Iris was right and the Black Swans showed up after all? Agent Jack was spying for BeauTek—for Opal's mom. Did he even know about Opal? Would he let her get away with brainwashing all those powerless kids? Would he actually help Opaline?!

Then he is absosmurfly a bad guy! her head told her, although a lil' part of her heart refused to believe it.

Pondering these imponderables, Scarlet searched the clouds as she spun in circles. Maybe she was making herself dizzy, because it seemed as if the mist was coming closer. Closer . . . *Closer!* Like a smog monster from an old horror movie! She slowed down, steadied herself, and took a second look.

"Oh. Swell. No," she whispered.

Descending from the sky, far too low to be normal, was a thick oblong cloud. Its millions of minuscule droplets glinted in the gray daylight like dirty diamond chips. Any moment now, it would land right on the grass of Scarlet's backyard! She backed up toward her house but couldn't tear her eyes away from the sight. It seemed to puff and steam like a living, breathing beast! A whole new bunch of even more imponderable imponderables filled Scarlet's head. Opaline's birthday brainwash-a-thon suddenly became the least of her worries, since she was about to be ABDUCTED BY ALIENS! In a ghostly, cloud-shaped spaceship!

Candace warned us about this! Scarlet thought, her feet suddenly tap-dancing in panic. *About being PROBED!*

She watched in wide-eyed terror, statue-still above the waist, shuffle-stepping below, as the shimmering smog floated just over the lawn. *Klick!* she heard, then *berzunk!* then *jeewhirrr!* And a stubby stairway stuck out like a metallic tongue, straight from the middle of the mist.

Scarlet was dancing as fast as she could. In place. *I won't let them take me without a fight!* she vowed, clenching her fists. But she couldn't seem to flee.

"Scarlet!" The hissed command came from the misty spaceship. "Get in the cloud!"

Scarlet always figured aliens would speak their own weird language, like Klingon or Na'vi or Shyriiwook. (*If, like Scarlet, you have three older brothers, you might know about those, too.*) But maybe the aliens had already tricked her mind into understanding them!

"Scarlet!" The order came again, in a voice that sounded

eerily familiar. "Get. In. The Cloud!" Maybe the aliens had tricked her mind into thinking they were *friends*!

"SCARLET!" Iris's face popped out of the mist, her purple ringlets bright against the wavery gray vapors. "C'mon!'

Scarlet stared skeptically. "How do I know you're not just an alien *disguised* as Iris?" she asked.

Iris rolled her eyes. "Catch!" she said. And the next thing Scarlet knew, a lollipop flew through the air. Cinnamon-flavored. She caught it just as she heard her mother calling for her from inside the house. And finally she managed to move her feet forward, tap-dancing toward the fog and up the three steps into the cloudship.

Jeewhirrr, berzunk, klick! The stairway folded up behind her and the cloud floated up into the sky. Down below, Scarlet could see her mother standing in the backyard, scanning the lawn, shaking her head, hands on her hips.

Giving the lollipop a hesitant lick, Scarlet took in her surroundings. Candace sat in the pilot's seat, steering. At first Scarlet thought she was wearing some sort of futuristic metal headset; then she realized it was just the silver sporks sticking out of her hair. Iris was buckled into the seat beside her. Behind them, Cheri brushed the knots out of Darth's tail. At her feet were bags of clothes, a small jar of purple cream, and a mangled mess of holiday lights.

"Explain," Scarlet said simply, taking a seat and strapping herself in. The spicy cinnamon candy stung her lips. But not in an unpleasant way.

Candace glanced over her shoulder, tilting the gearshift as she did, and the cloudship tipped a bit to the side. "Sugarsticks," she muttered, righting the craft again. "Still getting the hang of this thang!"

"But where did it come from?" Scarlet asked.

"I built it," Candace said, swerving to pass a gaggle of gingham geese. They honked back at her for cutting them off.

"You built . . ." Scarlet strung out the words ". . . a spaceship."

"Ever since I officially finished high school two years early, I've had a lot of free time," Candace remarked. "After I'd successfully launched the MAUVe satellite, the next logical step was a load-bearing airborne vehicle."

"That load being us," Cheri said.

"So you just *built* a *spaceship*?" Scarlet repeated in disbelief.

Cheri giggled. "Candace, we thought you were acting spacey because you were dating an astronaut."

"Very funny, Cheri." Candace adjusted a dial on the dashboard. "Building a spaceship is infinitely more probable. As long as you adhere to the basic principles of aerodynamics."

"Lift, thrust, gravity, and drag," Cheri quipped. "Lift coefficient times density times velocity squared, divided by two, multiplied by span, for example, to take off."

Scarlet sucked on the hot cinnamon lollipop. "If you say so," she said at last. "But what's up with the misty stuff?"

"Oh, that was my idea!" Iris chimed in, pivoting around in her copilot seat. "When we were texting yesterday, I had this vision that the best way to sneak up on Opaline would be as a cloud! Because she's always making clouds, you know? With her weird electrical storm powers?"

"Uh-huh . . ." Scarlet said.

"So I sketched out a design, sent it to Candace, and then she covered the spaceship with a zillion tiny prisms. Like on a mirrorball!"

"That way we're practically invisible," Candace explained while rubbing condensation off the windshield with the sleeve of her sweater. "The prisms reflect their surroundings, so you can't see the spaceship itself."

"And Candace built it so that the ventilation system recycles moisture in the atmosphere," Cheri added. "All those tiny fog particles are actually exhaust fumes."

"Glittering over the zillion tiny prisms!" Iris grinned.

"Right . . ." Scarlet said, letting it all sink in. "So we're flying around in the sky in an environmentally friendly disco cloud?"

"Totally!" Iris and Cheri nodded together.

Scarlet was silently impressed. Candace could sometimes be bumbling on the surface, but there was no doubt the erstwhile babysitter was a genuine teenius underneath. (*It's been a while since the last "erstwhile," so it found a spot to sneak back into the story.*)

"I had this sudden realization," Candace said, steering their cloud between towers toward the center of Sync City, "that Opal is going to override the brain circuitry of all your classmates at this birthday party of hers!"

Iris raised her eyebrows as Cheri shook her head. But since Candace had just swooped in on a homemade spaceship to get them, Scarlet resisted the urge to say, "*We* told *you* that!" She thought it, though.

"That's why I had to prism-break you out of being grounded," Candace continued, oblivious. "Because only the Ultra Violets can stop Opaline and save Sync City from a roving band of zombotomized students!"

"You mean we're crashing the party like we planned after all?" Scarlet said hopefully.

Cheri pointed to the bags at her feet. "Outfits!" she said, excited.

"We shall roll in on a cloud," Candace declared dramatically, "like the Greeks rode in on the Trojan horse!"

Confused, Scarlet said under her breath, "Is that from *Percy Jackson*?"

"Dunno!" Iris whispered back. "I'm only on the first book!"

22

Unfashionably Unfabulous

YOU KNOW HOW, IN THOSE MOVIES THAT ARE SNOTTILY slammed as "chick flicks," there's always a fashion montage? A scene when the heroine(s) scramble(s) to try on ton(s) of different outfit(s), in (s)earch of ju(s)t the right one for (s)ome (s)pecial occa(s)ion?

This is that scene! But in a book! With lots of exclamation points!!!

And utterly contrary.

Utterly contrary because nothing is ever quite what you'd expect it to be in the UV universe. Were that this *was* a chick flick, the girls would be dressing up in outfits, each one more fabulous than the last, until they found the most fierce *ensembles* ever! But the Ultra Violets were planning to crash Opaline's brainwash-a-rama. And Opaline did not exactly embrace fabulousness. She wore her shirts buttoned all the way up to the top, all the time. Her lightning-bolt tracksuit had become a kind of uniform. And her whole goal for her birthday party was to bring everybody down, down, down.

To stop Opaline, the Ultra Violets needed to sneak into this bummer of a downfest. Uninvited. Unnoticed. *Un*fabulous.

Yes, the Ultra Violets had to get dressed in the most blecch, boring, eww, yuck outfits they had never worn in their entire lives. In *ensemblahs*!

It was not going to be easy.

But if they had to go uggo to finally Get-O, Plan UF— UnFabulous—then that's what they would do for the sake of the students of Sync City.

"No tutu?" Scarlet asked, rifling through the musty old clothes Cheri had hung up on the cloudship's handy garment rack.

"No tutu," Iris said solemnly. "No sparkly gloss, either, Cheri."

Cheri stuck her lip out in a pout, but she didn't complain. Instead, she concentrated on chipping off the lilac and black nail polish she'd just painted yesterday.

"Okay then," Scarlet said with determination, wriggling out of her tutu. "Let's rock this."

Utterly contrary montage time!

While Candace commanded the cloudship, the changing of the clothes commenced. The three girls tried on one ugly outfit after another, prancing around and tossing T-shirts and scarves and sandals and once, by accident, Darth, between them. Scarlet settled on a polyester tangerine leisure suit

with pointy lapels on the jacket collar and bell-bottom cuffs on the pants. Cheri buttoned up bunches of hideous holiday cardigans, the most horrifying being one of a red-cheeked reindeer in a red felt Santa cap with a cottonball beard and a jingle bell for a nose. Iris dove into a tie-dyed turquoise muumuu with massive shoulder pads. It took her so long to find the neckhole, she felt like she was swimming in a sea of fabric.

The three girls paused to gawk at each other's outfits.

"Ewww!" they all wailed together, making ick-faces. "These clothes are so nasty!"

Candace looked back at them through the rearview mirror and burst out laughing. "OMV," she said, "if we weren't being all top-secret in our cloudship, I would totally post that photo on Smashface."

"Don't you dare!" Cheri demanded, jingling all the way. "If my mother hated my catsuit at the FLab, imagine what she'd say about all these funky rags from grandma's closet!"

"Well, FYI, I am not Smashface friends with your moms, Cher," Candace said, still chuckling. "But seriously, girls, the idea is to *blend in*. If you go to Opal's party dressed like that, you'll stand out!"

"We'll win the Worst Dressed award!" Iris griped, and who could argue with her massive shoulder pads? They were the ultimate in bossy.

"Then this is what not to wear, either," Scarlet agreed.

Utterly contrary montage take two! The girls modeled a whole new round of uggo outfits.

This time, when they were done changing, they were in no way sparkly, purple, super, or ultra. Nor were they car-crash-causingly hideous like before.

They were just three plain Janes in three baggy tracksuits.

yawn

"Does your grandma go to the gym a lot?" Scarlet asked, zipping up her hoodie.

"Only to use the sauna," Cheri shrugged.

"Wait, one finishing touch," Iris said as she looked them over. The tracksuits were old and faded, but their sporty colors were still noticeable. With a few superpowered tweaks, Iris turned them all to beige.

"There!" she said, satisfied with the makeunders. "You can't get more bland than that!"

Cheri was just reaching for her Hello Kitty bling ring amongst the pile of discarded clothes when the glimmer of its rhinestones caught Iris's eye. "Nuh-uh, Cher," she stopped her. "Too glamorous!"

Cheri sighed, ever so slightly irked, and slipped the ring to Darth for safekeeping. He put it on his tail. "Okay, RiRi," she said, speaking in a tone of voice she usually saved for her mother. It was especially unnatural for Cheri to be unfabulous, and for a moment in that beige tracksuit, she almost forgot who she was. She knew true fabulousness was something you had in your heart, no matter what clothes you were wearing or whether you'd blown out your hair or not. She just preferred her outer and inner divas to match. Which reminded her . . .

"Hey, Iris," Cheri asked, "aren't you forgetting about something, too?"

Iris frowned. She had not forgotten. She was just putting it off as long as possible . . .

"Ten seconds till touchdown, girls!" Candace called. "Buckle up again!"

"Here goes," Iris said as she took her seat. Then she wrapped a purple ringlet around one of her pinkie fingers, closed her eyes for just a second or three . . .

And when she opened them again, her hair was a nearly

normal color. A blah, dull, dishwater dirty blond. Almost as beige as her tracksuit.

But if you looked at it close enough, in the light of a sunbeam, you just might notice the faintest hint, the faintest tint, of violet.

Scary Smileys

THE GIRLS WATCHED AS THE GLITTERING CLOUDSHIP wafted back up to the sky, the last traces of mist evaporating around them and the moisture giving Iris's blah blond curls an extra kink. Soon it was impossible to spot Candace's aircraft among all the actual clouds in the sky.

Standing outside Tom's Diner in their bland beige tracksuits, the (*shhh!*) Ultra Violets barely attracted a second glance. And that felt surprisingly strange. Not long ago (*page 94, specifically*), Cheri had bemoaned not being "an oblivio" anymore. Now, in disguise, incognito, they at least looked the part. No one stopped to do a double take at Iris's wild purple hair or Scarlet's poofy red tutu—although a dull tracksuit couldn't keep her from rabbiting up and down in *petit changements*. Cheri's computery superpowers were rarely on display, anyway, but she just felt strange because she'd never dressed this boring before.

"Honestly," Cheri said, "acting oblivio is kind of a drag, alas."

"Quoth the raven, totally," Scarlet joked. "I'd way rather play Little Orphan Annie."

"Let's deal with this downer party so that we can get back to being viomazing," Iris agreed.

The three (*silence, please!*) Ultra Violets quickly touched pinkies, a small solar flare sparking from their fingertips. Then Scarlet fanned her fingers out like a firework explosion, whispering, "Ka-pow!"

Cheri smiled. "Blammo!" she added between air quotes. Darth popped up out of his bag to make air quotes, too.

"Or how about 'shazam!'?" Iris winked.

Ironic superhero sound effects out of their systems, they walked into Tom's Diner.

Opaline's party was being held in the back room. Iris, Cheri, and Scarlet, even in their meh tracksuits, didn't want to risk strolling right in until they'd checked what was up. So they each took a seat at the counter. It was the perfect spot for spying—they could see through to the party room, but the kitchen grill was in between. Lots of pretty cake pedestals decorated the countertop, good for hiding behind, too.

"Red velvet," Scarlet drooled, her nose pressed up against the closest cake dome. "Yum!"

"Cake later!" Cheri said in a hush, peeking out above a menu.

"Well look who it is!" The sassy voice shocked the girls straight on their stools, and they whipped their heads around in unison to face the beehived waitress. Her streaky Franken-bouffant appeared to be a full foot higher than the last time they'd seen it, and Cheri wondered just how much hairspray the woman had to use to keep the towering 'do in place. She probably went through a bottle a day.

The waitress leaned one elbow against the countertop, sizing up the girls as she snapped her gum. "Something's different about you three amigas . . ." She peered from Scarlet to Cheri to Iris, lingering for a moment on her curls. "But I can't put my finger on what."

"We've just come from an extremely beige track practice," Cheri bluffed. "That's probably it."

"Extreme sports are all the beige now, you know," Iris added.

"Nope!" The waitress clapped her hands sharply, causing the girls to sit up even straighter. "Kiss my grits if that ain't it. But whatever it is . . ."

The girls braced themselves, hoping the beehived waitress wouldn't blow their cover.

". . . betcha I've got your order!" She slapped her little notepad against her plump hip, not jotting down a thing. "Butterbeer, heavy on the sauce, for you, Spunky Brewster. Strawberry milkshake for Princess. And triple berry parfait for Miss Artsy Fartsy, am I right?"

The trio was actually too nervous to taste a thing, and Iris was completely appalled to be described as "fartsy," even if it was only an easy rhyme, and yet . . .

"We can't just sit here and not order," Scarlet muttered through her teeth.

"Right!" Iris said out loud, flashing the most artless smile she could imagine. "Awesome memory!"

"That's 'cause I'm like an elephant, hon," the waitress said with a confidential nod of her bouffant. "I forgive, but I never forget." Then she spun on the heel of her orthopedic sneakers and sashayed off to get their order.

"*Awk-weird!*" Scarlet sang under her breath. Something about the tension of the moment set her quivering with the silent giggles—which four out of five doctors agree are highly contagious. Iris bit the inside of her cheeks to stop herself from starting. Cheri pinched her earlobe, hard. Scarlet gave herself one of those thumps on the shoulder. And burped.

"Gross, Scarlet!" Cheri said, pinching her nose with her free hand while Darth fanned the air with his tail.

"At least I'm not 'fartsy'!" Scarlet teased.

"Please," Iris begged. "That is *so* not funny." Even though it was a little bit funny. The silent giggles went viral again, but the sight of the beehived waitress returning with their order quieted them down.

Hidden behind cake stands and menus, frosted butterbeer mugs and tall parfait glasses, the (*hush your mouth, child!*) Ultra Violets spied past the grizzled fry cook at the grill to the party room beyond. If they hadn't already recovered from their giggle fit, what they saw would have cured them stat!

Bloated brown balloons with yellow smiley faces covered the back wall. A few smiley face balloons might have been cute. But there must have been a hundred of them. And these smiley faces were custom-designed with a black lightning zigzag between the eyes. Row upon row upon row upon row beamed forth, bobbing dumbly like an entire audience that had already been hypnotized by Opaline. Iris spotted one in the corner that had lost its air: Yellow and brown, it hung from the wall like a rotting banana, one withered dot eye drooping lower than the other, the thick line of its smile ripply as a worm.

"Those balloons are freaking me out," Scarlet said, swallowing a big gulp of her butterbeer.

In the middle of the balloons hung a banner proclaiming, It's the Big 1-2! Opal sat beneath it on a plump seat cushioned with the same red vinyl that was used on all the diner's stools and booths. It was probably supposed to be a birthday throne. But it reminded Iris of the *shudder* dentist's chair.

For her special day, Opal had spruced up her typical tracksuit uniform with some special touches: Both the lightning bolt across her chest and the Peter Pan collar around her neck were cut from slick patent leather in a sickening acid yellow. The shade reminded Iris of something. But the same way the beehived waitress hadn't been able to figure out what was different about Iris, neither could Iris—kiss her grits?!— recall why that acid yellow felt so queasily familiar.

Where have I seen that color before? Iris asked herself.

Opal's mom, Dr. Trudeau, crouched in a corner, snapping photos while guarding a small side table. It was covered with goody bags in the same bilious shade.

Something about that toxic chartreuse . . . Iris thought.

But she couldn't let herself be distracted by the curious yellow now. Another sight was much more disturbing.

Slumped in seats throughout the party room was most of the sixth grade. The students had their backs to the girls, but they could still recognize them. Martin. Albert. Emma. The Jensen twins. Swaying ever so slightly, they stared up at the wall of scary smileys. Every now and then, one would moan, *"Mnoh!"* and claw at the air, grasping for something that wasn't there.

Whenever that happened, K-Liz slapped their hands down with a crack of her scaly tail.

"Sugarsticks!" Scarlet spat. "Opal's already short-circuited the whole class!"

"Maybe not the *whole* class," Iris murmured back. "Look!"

Standing in single file, clutching gifts, were a few more students. From the sidelines, BellaBritney cheered them on, pointing the way with her pathetic pompom—and blocking all the zombos from view. The (*shut up already!*) Ultra Violets looked on with dread as Rachel Wright reached the front of the line.

Opaline snapped her fingers.

Beckoned Rachel closer, cupping her hand like she had a secret to share.

And as soon as Rachel got near enough, Opal licked her pinkie finger and stuck it in her ear!

Small sparks shot out as Opaline's electric volts raced straight into her victim's brain. When she was done, Rachel stumbled away, her ear charred black like a burnt cauliflower.

Then K-Liz directed the newest slave to a seat while Opaline tossed her latest birthday present onto the pile beside her throne.

"An electric wet willy!" Scarlet pounded her fist on the countertop, making all the cakes clatter on their pedestals. "Of all the lowdown dirty tricks!"

Iris didn't say anything. She just stared at the end of Opal's receiving line. The blue of her eyes drained to pale.

Cheri and Scarlet followed her gaze. There, top hat in hand, stood Sebastian. Iris could see the colorful beads of her friendship bracelet dangling around his wrist.

Douglas and Malik stood in line, too, hoverboards at their feet.

"Girls?" Iris whispered.

She didn't have to say anything else.

Cheri hurried to put some change on the counter and pick up Darth in her bag. Then the (*no*, you *shut up!*) Ultra Violets slipped off their stools and stole toward the swinging doors to the private party room.

As the beehived waitress went to clear their glasses, she paused, watching the girls go. Iris was last of the three, her ringlets bouncing behind her. "*That* was it!" the waitress said to nobody but herself. "She changed her hair color." The waitress pocketed the cash, mumbling, "A little young to be dealing with roots, if you ask me."

Roots?

At the tips, Iris's curly strands were still the blah beigey blond she'd switched it to. With just a hint of violet.

But at the crown of her head, already, the hair was turning back to full-on purple.

L'Eau No Again!

IT WAS THE QUIETEST PARTY-CRASH EVER. *SO QUIET IT* *whispered like this.* In their blergh tracksuits, defrocked of all things sparkly and/or bright, the girls almost blended into the paneling. They were just sneaking toward the end of Opal's receiving line when Dr. Trudeau sprang up from her crouch. She peered across the room, her nostrils twitching like an inquisitive gopher's.

"She's staring right at us!" Cheri gasped. "Do you think she'll recognize me minus the gloss?" she asked, biting her lower lip.

Just then, the doors behind them swung open with a vigorous hip bump by the beehived waitress. She strutted straight past the Ultra Violets, all her concentration on the blazing cake she was balancing atop a glass pedestal. Tongues of flame licked up from it, coming dangerously close to her bouffant. Considering it was probably coated with an entire can of hairspray, she was a towering inferno waiting to happen.

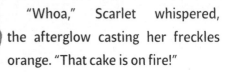

"Whoa," Scarlet whispered, the afterglow casting her freckles orange. "That cake is on fire!"

Reflected flames danced in Iris's eyes. She watched as the waitress put the burning dessert down on a table, then turned around and hotfooted it out of the room again.

As she left, she reached up to stamp out a small brushfire that had sparked in her bouffant just above her ear.

"Okay, children!" Dr. Trudeau called out as Opal protested "*Mom!*" over her. Dr. Trudeau carried on anyway.

"*Hap-py Birth-day to You!*" she sang, gesturing for all the kids to join in.

"*Hap-py Birth-day O+2!*" BellaBritney bellowed, the goth half of her yanking down the cheer half's raised pompom.

"*Hurhbeezsmlurfhay dur Ohpulrgh,*" the zombotomized guests moaned.

"Huh?" Scarlet said, crossing her eyes at the craziness.

"I think that's the zombo translation of the song," Iris deadpanned while Dr. Trudeau rallied to the big finish.

"*Hap-py Birth-day to You!*" she crooned. "How old are you now, honey?"

"Oh please," Opal sniped, sliding down from her shiny red ~~dentist chair~~ throne. "Like you don't know." Shoving past her mother, she stood behind the blazing cake and before her brain-fried guests.

"It's your favorite, Opal," her mother said, stretching her arm out to give her a hug, but hesitating. The fire highlighted the frown lines on her face. "Peach Melba flambé with crème du brussels sprout sauce."

Watching from their corner spot, Scarlet stuck out her tongue. Ick-facing back, Iris whispered, "That has *got* to be the least awesome sauce ever."

Iz stinkz like her purfoom, Darth thought, peeking out of Cheri's tote bag.

"Yeah," Cheri said, "all it's missing is a dash of sweat socks!"

At the cake table, K-Liz sidled up to Opal, her forked tongue flicking in anticipation. "Quick!" she hissed. "Make a wisssh and blow it out."

"Before it—yay!—burns away!" BellaBritney jumped up and down, her cheer half getting the best of her goth half for a moment. But just a moment. "Let it burn," Goth Bella intoned somberly, "and then we can eat the ashes that symbolize our ravaged youth."

239

Ignoring BellaBritney's tasteless comment, Opal leaned over the still-flaming cake. But she didn't suck in a big breath to blow out the fire. She just stared at it, small orange embers kindling in her brown eyes. Suddenly, out of thin air, a teeny-tiny storm cloud formed just above it. Like a ceiling sprinkler in a burning building, it doused the blaze with a quick shower.

The dazed party guests slow-clapped. The applause was not sarcastic-slow. Just sad. Opal didn't seem to care. She beamed at her ~~future servants~~ school friends. Then she picked up a gleaming silver cake knife and brandished it above her head.

"O sit!" she ordered.

Instantly, all the already-zombotomized students slunk lower in their chairs. The other guests—the few still in the line, and in their right minds—scrambled to find seats. The Ultra Violets grabbed the last three in the back: Scarlet using Iris's messenger bag to give herself a boost so that she could still see; Iris slouching down so she wouldn't stand out. Her glance fell upon the back of Sebastian's neck, the cute way his ears stuck out just a little, the cool way his hair started off short and tapered at the nape and then got shaggier and more tousleable toward the top. (*Ahem, Iris! Now is not the time for crushing on a boy!*)

"Before I cut the cake," Opaline said to the crowd, lowering the knife again, "I want you all to know that this is no ordinary birthday party."

"*Nokidding!*" Scarlet coughed, waving aside some smoke that had drifted back their way.

"At *my* birthday party," Opal continued, the wall of creepy smiley balloons nodding behind her, "all of *you* are going to leave with a present!"

As the guests groaned with excitement, Opal swung her arm in her trademark circle, snapping her fingers twice. Like hostesses on a game show, BellaBritney and K-Liz skipped behind her. Each grabbed a corner of the It's the Big 1-2! banner and pulled it down like a window shade. Opal pressed an icon on her smartphone, and a strange animated poster appeared on the unfurled screen.

In stark black, white, and yellow, it showed a graphic illustration of Opal. Her hair was precisely parted and pulled back tight. In the center of her forehead, a small lightning bolt struck, again and again and again. Her eyes spiraled, swirling chocolate and vanilla and orangey-peach. One eyebrow was sharply arched. On the side opposite it, one corner of her mouth smirked.

Maybe it was supposed to be a smile.

But it just looked like a smirk.

And in her hand, the Opaline poster girl held some kind of small cannonball. But instead of a lighted fuse, like you'd see in cartoons, the bomb had one of those poufs you squeeze to spray perfume. In rhythm with the *zzzt-zzzt-zzzt* of Opal's blinking lightning bolt, the bomb *spritz-spritz-spritz*ed perfume. Underneath the animated picture, in big block letters, it said:

L'EAU d'OPES

"*L'eau?*" Cheri whispered. "As in French for perfume?"

"L'oh Dopes?" Scarlet sounded it out.

"L'eau no!" Iris said, putting it together. "It's Opaline's perfume!"

P-ew, Darth thought, and not for the first time. *Smelz bad 4 u.*

"So that's the present?" Scarlet grimaced. "Opal's funky stank?"

"I think we're about to find out," Iris answered, anxiously tugging on one of her fake-beigey tendrils.

"Students of Chronic Prep," Opaline said, while her mother stood by, puffed up with pride and snapping photos. "Are you feeling kind of blue?"

"*Myneah*," the zombos agreed listlessly—although Goth Bella sighed with contentment, her half of her face splitting into a smile.

"Too much homework bringing you down?" Opal prompted.

"Way down!" Albert shouted, his eyes strangely vacant and his face flushed with rage. Watching him out of the corner of her eye, Cheri winced. Albert was captain of the mathletes. He *lived* for homework! Or at least he used to . . .

"Worried you don't have any *friends*?" Opal taunted. "Any forever-and-ever besties you can call your own?"

Iris's blood ran cold. She was sure Opaline hadn't spotted them, in the back of the room in their beige camo. But still Iris felt that the sharp barb in Opal's question was somehow aimed straight at her.

"*Mmmnurgh!*" the zombotomized guests moaned in their seats. Some of them gnashed their teeth. Others clawed at the air. Zombo Emma gnawed on her thumbnail.

Zombo Rachel started to sob. Even Sebastian looked stressed, running his hand through his hair. It grew so quiet in the party room that the only sounds to be heard were the *whirs* from Dr. Trudeau's camera phone and the occasional squeak when one balloon rubbed against another.

Iris looked closer at the scary smileys. Something was different about them. Something was changing. It wouldn't have been noticeable to the naked eye. But Iris's infraviolet vision suddenly perceived mold-green vapors seeping from the balloons. Out of the eerie lightning bolts between the dot eyes. Ever so slowly, they were all leaking . . . air?

Opal continued with her speech. "Maybe most important of all"—she dropped her voice and leaned forward, speaking out over her rapidly melting Peach Melba brussels sprout birthday cake—"do you never . . ."

She let the question hang in the air for a few seconds.

". . . ever . . ." she said, a little bit louder now.

". . . EVER . . ." she repeated in a shout, electric currents crackling off her shoulders ". . . WANT TO HAVE B.O.?"

Zombo Julie shrieked in terror. Zombo Abby fainted into her plate, a slice of cold pizza her pillow. Malik subtly lifted his elbows and sniffed his armpits to check. The entire room erupted into murmurs about the dual menaces: too much homework and rampant sweat.

"Students of Chronic Prep," Opal

244

said again when the furor had finally died down. "And special guests . . ." she added, glancing over in the direction of Sebastian, Douglas, and Malik. She gave the boys a flirty wink that made Iris's hair curl even curlier. "I'm here to tell you," Opal oozed, "that you're never going to have to worry about any of that stuff again."

By this point in Opal's oration, Scarlet had been kicking her chair leg with the back of her heel so hard that it dented in. The seat dipped dangerously to one side, and like a gymnast on a pommel horse, Scarlet had to push herself up on her arms just to keep from sliding off.

Opal had paused for dramatic effect, dipping a pinkie into her cake and scooping up a dollop of cabbagey green cream. "You won't have to worry," she went on, licking her finger, "because you guys are all getting the gift of—"

"*Lohhhhhhhhh Dopes!*" BellaBritney cut her off with a drawn-out cheer. For once her two sides were in agreement, shaking the solitary pompom with both hands.

Miffed that BellaBritney had stolen her thunder, Opal aimed that same pinkie, still coated with brussels sprout sauce. And she shot a razor-blade lightning bolt straight at the pompom, shearing it in half. The sliced-off plastic fringe fell to the floor like dry needles from a dead pine tree.

"Gimme a *wah*," BellaBritney moped, now as bummed out as all the rest of the zombos.

"Yes, my signature scent," Opal announced, back in command. "L'eau d'Opes. Perfume for the girls. Aftershave for the boys! All it takes is a lil' spritz, and sadness? Gone-*o*. Homework? Forget *o*-bout it. Friends? Thousands *o'* them, f*o*-ever!"

At the sound of *lil'*, Scarlet's ears perked up, and she whipped her head around so fast that her own licorice-stick-straight ponytail hit her smack in the eyes. They began to water. She blinked furiously to clear them, tears from the sting trickling down her cheeks. But she couldn't wipe her eyes without lowering herself back down on the broken chair. She'd thought she'd detected some movement, a disruption, somewhere in the crowd. By the time she could see again, she couldn't be sure.

"L'eau d'Opes!" Opal was wrapping up her speech, bobbing her head in time with the leaking lightning-bolt smileys. "Breathe it in and troubles begone!" she said. Off to the side, Dr. Trudeau mouthed the words along with her daughter, even acting them out with controlled waves of her hands. Using urgent little jabs, she pointed to her mouth. "Oh, right," Opal said, taking the hint. "And bonus! It'll keep your breath minty-fresh, too!"

"*Mmnrawrs!*" Zombo Brad roared, then began pounding his table like a caveman. "O-Dopes! O-Dopes! O-Dopes!" The rest of the zombos picked up the chant. They moaned and groaned so loud, the sound squished the slowly deflating smiley balloons against the wall.

Standing over the peach melba brussels sprout birthday cake, Opal savored the moment. It was a pretty perfect party. The entire class was shouting her name. Pledging their allegiance to her. As her dopes! Now it wasn't just K-Liz and BellaBritney: She had tons of followers. Real kids, too, not mutant freaks. *So what if I had to numb them all with nerve gas perfume and short-circuit their brains to get them?* she bickered with the doubting voice in her mind. But even the shouts of all those kids couldn't silence it.

To shake it off, Opal jerked her head from one shoulder to the other, static electricity crackling through her brown bob. With all the strength she could summon, she swung her arm in the widest circle possible, snapping up high, snapping down low. Sparks shot out as her fingers clicked, and the kids at the party shut up.

Dr. Trudeau scuttled to her daughter's side, a glass perfume bomb big as a basketball tucked under her arm. A greenish-gray liquid

sloshed around inside it. Just like on the poster, the bottle had a poufy atomizer embellished with an acid-yellow tassel. Dr. Trudeau gave it a single pump, and an oily mist filled the air, evaporating into the same moldy vapors Iris had spotted seeping out of the balloons. "Everyone gets a spritz before they leave!" she promised. "Right after we serve the cake—and the birthday girl finishes with her, er, receiving line. Right, honey? I think there are a few kids you still haven't, ah, 'said thank you' to."

"I know, Mom!" Opal rolled her eyes and climbed back onto the birthday throne while Dr. Trudeau put down the perfume bomb and held up one of the sulfurous yellow goody bags. She swung it back and forth, back and forth. The zombos swayed along. "And nobody forget to take home a fun-size party favor!" Dr. Trudeau chimed. "The first sample of L'eau d'Opes is free." Then, in a rushed voice, running all her words together, she added: "Use code OPAL12 for a two-percent discount in stores or online first-time customers only not to be combined with any other offers shipping and handling extra certain restrictions apply. And no returns accepted."

No Returns! Iris's eyes popped open. *That's where I've seen those yellow bags before—the Mall of No Returns!*

"L'eau d'Opes is not just phony aromatherapy, guys," Iris hissed to Scarlet and Cheri. "I think it's some kind of airborne poison! From BeauTek! That stinky perfume Opal's been wearing must be what's bringing everyone down— lowering their resistance so that she can rewire their brains! And those scary balloons are full of it!"

Like I sezd, Darth thought, though only Cheri could hear him, *sumting's rotten.*

Sticky Stuff

THE CLASS OF CHRONIC PREP SHORT-CIRCUITED INTO
slaves. A trio of punk-rock Graffiti Boys curious about a cure-all aftershave. Three supergirls in the ugliest beige tracksuits you have ever seen. And a wall of balloons leaking toxic perfume. That's the "Previously On" of *The Ultra Violets # 2: Power to the Purple!*

So now what?

That's exactly what the Ultra Violets were asking themselves.

"So now what?" Scarlet said. (*See, told ya.*)

"IDK," Iris fretted, her eyes darting across the room. Opal's mom was spooning out the melted Peach Melba into soup bowls. K-Liz trailed behind her, a pitcher of crème du brussels sprout sauce gripped by her tail. She drizzled it on top of

the melty ice cream and cake whether or not a guest asked for it—which even the zombos didn't. And back on her vinyl diner throne, Opal held a tankard of her birthday dessert in one hand, taking sips through a bendy straw as she prepared to dole out the last of the electric wet willies with the other.

"Opal's mom said everyone would get a baddy bag at the *end* of the party," Iris deliberated, "but this whole room is filling up with the poison perfume as we speak, weakening anyone Opal hasn't zombofied yet. So let's start by stopping the electroshocks, to spare whoever's still okay." *Including Sebastian,* Iris thought, her heart pounding. *How can I save him from Opal and still keep the mystery alive?*

Keeping that particular worry to herself, Iris looked from Cheri to Scarlet to see if they agreed about cutting the power first. But neither one said anything. They just stared back at her. Like they were the deer and she was the headlights. Then Scarlet gulped hard enough for Iris to hear, and Cheri fumbled frantically in her tote bag. She pulled out a small mirror and, cupping it in the palm of her hand, held it up to Iris.

"OMV," Iris whispered, slinking down even deeper in her seat.

The mirror didn't lie. Iris's long ringlets were still dull lavender blond at the ends. But the entire top half of her hair had turned back to deep purple.

"What happened?" Cheri said, finally finding some words. "Can you change it to blond again?"

251

"I don't think so!" Iris replied, desperate. "For some reason my purple hair is the only thing I can't seem to colorize, at least not for long!"

"How ironic," Scarlet muttered. "Guess the ka-pow's on us!" Then she reached forward, and for a split second Iris didn't know *what* Scarlet was going to do—pull her hair? How would that help?! But Scarlet just said, "Yoink!" And yanked up the hood of Iris's tracksuit.

"Oh, right," Iris breathed, shoving the bulk of her hair into it. The beige hoodie really was not a festive party look, and she felt a bit like a monk in sweatpants. But what choice did she have?

"That's it; I can't take it anymore!" Cheri balked. She passed the mirror back to Darth, who had her tube of lip gloss at the ready. Cheri rolled on a sheer layer of sticky lilac glitter before Iris or Scarlet could stop her. "Sorry," she said once the deed was done. "But if we're about to take down this party, I've got to be feeling it, you know?"

"I hear that," Iris sighed, rolling her eyes at her ridiculous hood.

Iris said it in sympathy. But Cheri took it as a cue. With a few expert dabs, she dotted some gloss on Iris's and Scarlet's lips, too.

"*So* much better!" Cheri smiled, while Iris's and Scarlet's sparkly mouths fell open in surprise. "Purple is the CCF!"

"CCF?" Scarlet repeated.

"Coolest Color Forever," Iris guessed, spelling out the letters. "It really does go with everything."

"C'mon guys, makeovers after, okay?" Scarlet pressed impatiently—even though the lilac lip gloss did look *terribly* pretty against her smoky gray eyes. She pulled up her own hood and tucked her ponytail inside. "It's time for Operation Get-O, Plan Whatever-Letter-of-the-Alphabet-We-Still-Have-Left!"

"'K!" Iris said. Because she agreed. And because they hadn't used that letter yet.

There in the corner of the back room of Tom's Diner, the Ultra Violets bowed their heads into a huddle and touched pinkie fingers again, powering up. Scarlet's bangs took on a distinctly aubergine glow. Cheri's berry-red waves flushed magenta. And beneath the cover of her beige hood, Iris's curls shone ultraviolet.

"Polymer, please?" Iris asked Cheri, who was reluctantly cramming her own hair into the hood of her tracksuit.

From the tote bag, Darth passed up the jar with the purple cream. If you didn't know any better, you'd think it was just another pot of lip gloss. But it wasn't. Iris popped the lid and scooped out a gummy plummy glob. Then she slipped her hand inside her hood, making a mini-ick-face as she grabbled around underneath it.

"Iris, are you sure you're sure about this?" Scarlet asked, getting to her feet. "It's risky! Can't I just cancan-kick Opaline across the river?"

"No way," Iris hissed, shoving her hands into the pockets of her hoodie. Heads down, the three girls shuffled toward the front of the line. "Then everybody would see your superstrength!"

"Right," Cheri added. "No one must know!"

Out of the corner of her eye, Iris noticed Opal's mom heading their way, her arms loaded up with Opal's presents. She brushed right past them and out the doors to the diner, not giving the girls a second glance.

"Well, if anything goes wrong," Scarlet continued, troubled, "then it's vio-clobbering time. And I won't care who sees!" She folded her arms and twisted her glitter-dusted lips into a tight knot to keep herself from saying anything else.

The three girls cut the line, just ahead of Sebastian, Douglas, and Malik.

It's not too late. Iris kept her head down. *I hope!*

"Oh, *excusez* us," Cheri said to the other kids behind them, "hope you don't mind! It's just that we're seriously late for an extremely beige soccer match, and we didn't know there was going to be a big speech about a wonder-perfume, and we wouldn't want to leave without giving the birthday girl our bestiest wishes, because that would be rude."

"Ruder than cutting in line?" some girl grumbled—clearly L'eau d'Opes was already poisoning *her* mood. A shot from Scarlet's gunpowder eyes struck her silent. But Douglas, the boy with the wispy sideburns—and therefore the boy most interested in a fun-size sample of aftershave—stared at Cheri, bedazed. Possibly because of the perfume, too. But probably because her emerald green eyes were so fresh. And her lip gloss was so glittery. Wait, didn't he know this girl from somewhere?

Cheri spun around to face front, bowing her head, too, so that the hoverboys wouldn't keep gaping at them.

And then Iris stepped up to Opaline.

Iris hardly dared look at her. As she focused her powers, her temperature started to skyrocket. She could feel her eyes beginning to blaze ultraviolet. "Happy birthday, Opaline," she whispered, in a voice she hoped was as bland as her tracksuit.

From her seat on the throne, sipping her brussels sprout sludge through her straw, Opal eyed the girl in the hood with suspicion. She couldn't quite see her face, but something about her seemed familiar. Or maybe she went to the same school as those hoverboys behind her?

Eh, Opal thought, happy to add another zombo to the crew. *The more the scarier!*

"C'mere," she whispered back, beckoning the girl closer. Her pinkie finger fizzed with electricity. "I've got a special birthday secret to share."

"Ooh, goody!" Iris cooed, trying to sound both stupid and excited as she adjusted her ultraviolet body temperature *just so*. And very, very, (very) carefully, keeping her hair hidden, she tucked the hood behind her ear and leaned in to "listen."

As she'd done with all the guests before, Opal gave her pinkie a lick. Then she stuck the sizzling digit into Iris's ear. But this time was different. This time . . .

"Yuck!" Opal yelped, yanking her finger out again. "What the—?"

Opal's pinkie was coated in a rubbery purple substance. A waxy polymer that just so happened to stop electric currents in their tracks (and certainly would have won first place in any science fair, thank you very much again, Iris's smartypants mom!). After Iris had filled her ear with the gummy plummy cream that the girls had concocted from their FLab shoplifting trip, she powered up her temperature for the catalytic conversion. And within just a second or three, it had hardened. Right onto Opal's lethal fingertip, wrapping around it like some sort of tiny chemical jellyfish!

The Ultra Violets had put a cap on Opaline's power pinkie. The electric wet willy portion of the party was so over.

As Opal spluttered, hopelessly shaking her hand, unable to get the goop off it, the Ultra Violets stepped out of line. Next on their to-undo list: the baddy bags. But one person—or rather two persons—or rather two halves of one person?!—blocked their way.

"Hey," Cheer Brit drawled uncertainly, while Goth Bella simply sneered. "Are you guys on pep squad? I don't recognize that school color . . ."

Cheri was just about to bluff some beigey answer—she'd gotten supergood at bluffing since the start of this story—while Scarlet and Iris snuck past. But then this happened: A long ringlet, 100 percent purple from root to tip, sprung straight out from beneath Iris's hood like a jack-in-the-box making a jailbreak. It was as if her hair had a mind of its own.

"Iris?" Sebastian said from his spot in the line.

"Iris!" Opal screamed, pointing an accusing electric finger. The purple rubber pinkie cap stopped the flow of the voltage, and all of Opal's frustrated energy circulated back into her nervous system. Sparks as long as snakes shot from her shoulders, and her hair stood completely on end.

Betrayed by her own tresses, Iris stood there, exposed. The Ultra Violets' cover had been blown.

Not Cute

OPALINE SLID OFF HER THRONE. SWINGING BACK HER hand, she shoved her tankard at one of her glum followers. Her backlogged electricity had made the glass so scalding hot that the kid immediately dropped it, and it shattered to pieces. Boiling brussels sprout sauce splashed all over the place, chunky driblets sizzling onto the lower rows of the scary smiley balloons and even staining Sebastian's best sneakers.

"Dude," he muttered, disgusted, and immediately hopped onto his hoverboard to keep off the sticky, stinky floor. His two buddies did the same.

Opal didn't care about the steaming brussels sprout puddle. She marched straight through it and up to Iris, her jaw clenched. Iris held her ground, hands on her hips, pale periwinkle eyes burning back at Opaline, who reached out with her rubbery pinkie and pushed off Iris's hood.

More ultraviolet than ever, Iris's curls burst out north, south, east, west, in every possible direction. Obviously her hair was happy—if hair has feelings—to be free again.

"Double-yoink," Scarlet mumbled, slowly pulling down her own hood. Her aubergine pony swished to and fro as she stood beside Iris. Next to her, Cheri ran her fingers through her magenta waves, hoping the hood hadn't flattened them.

"The Ultra Violets," Opal growled in a voice so low only the four girls could hear, "were NOT invited to this birthday party!"

"Alas, Opes, that was *très* mean of you!" Cheri exclaimed. "I know I turned down the role of evil brain in your, um, cute little O+2 thing, but still . . ."

"We are *not* 'cute'!" Opal barked—much to Cheer Brit's disappointment and Goth Bella's glee.

"I *completely* agree!" Cheri cried. Finally Opal was making some sense! Progress?

"You know, Opal"—Scarlet blew her black-purple bangs out of her eyes—"we actually had a whole ice-cream sandwich birthday party planned for you. That we had to cancel when you blew us off for this freak show!" (Wisely, Scarlet decided to leave out the part about their party doubling as an intervention.)

Opal quaked with fury. Electric yellow currents orbited around her, and tiny lightning bolts whizzed all over the place. The hum of her pent-up electricity enthralled her shocked followers, and they all shuffled closer, lowing like cattle at a fence. Opal swung back her good hand again, keeping the zombos at a distance. They huddled in the brussels sprout puddle beneath the pulsating L'eau d'Opes poster and the bobbing cult of balloons.

"Let me guess, the skunk sniffed me out," Opal said bitterly, her brown eyes overcast with storm clouds.

"*That*'s why you wanted Darth? Because you knew he'd smell the truth about your vile perfume?" Scarlet challenged.

"Because the Vi-Shush turned him into a bioweapon, too!" Cheri tightened her grasp on Darth's bag. "He did try to tell us," she admitted. "But we had to see it for ourselves!"

Opaline tossed her head, sending a fresh round of electrical charges into the balloons behind her. A few popped like bubble wrap, spitting their toxic fumes into the air. "Why can't you three, and your stanky little mascot, just leave me alone?" she snapped.

Iris shook her head like this was the saddest thing she'd ever heard. Even her curls drooped a smidge, like they were sad, too—*if* hair has feelings. "Opaline," she said, "you may not want to make up and be friends again—"

"Dur!" Opal interjected churlishly. She *hated* it when Iris called her by her full name. The way she said it made it sound so darn *sparkly*!

Iris ignored this. "But no way are we going to just stand by and watch while you fry the brains of our entire class!" *Or my sorta boyfriend,* she thought, also trying to ignore the fact that Sebastian was probably staring at her right now, glowing ultraviolet.

Opaline scoffed, leaning back a bit as K-Liz and BellaBritney flanked her sides. "Too little, too late, losers!" she smirked. As if to prove her point, all her electrocuted minions repeated, "*Toohlilootlayloozrz.*"

"We thought you might say that," Iris answered, with a cross between a shudder and a shrug. "Cher?"

Cheri had just been lifting Darth out of her tote bag. In stressful situations such as these, she found it helped to snuggle the soft little skunk. And stroking his fur protected her manicure, since it kept her from biting her nails. "Yes," she said, turning her attention back to the face-off. Her green eyes streamed with data as she stated, "We—well, I—calculated that if we channeled a mass transient variation of current, we could reverse the effects of your individuated electroshocking with a, um, single awesome solar event."

Opal scrunched her eyebrows together, struggling to process this information. With a crisp snap of her fingers, she ordered AI-bot Feinstein, her backup brain, to step forward. He tottered out from the crowd and stared at Cheri with empty eyes. She didn't think he even recognized her, not really. And *silent scream* he was wearing high-waisted, pleated-front khakis again, in total defiance of Cheri's original stealth makeover. Cheri had to turn away for a moment, so disturbing was the sight. "*The horror,*" she whispered, holding Darth close to shield him from the hideous pants. He'd already faced way too many terrors in his young skunk life. Cheri adamantly refused to expose him to this one.

"An impossible hypothesis," Albert droned. "To execute a surge of such magnitude on so many subjects simultaneously would require a mammoth generator. Or a private sun—"

"Check," Scarlet muttered under her breath, casting a sidelong glance at Iris.

"—and a multi-clamp jumper cable," Al-bot finished. Normally his glasses would have fogged up with the excitement of delivering such an airtight defense. But now he just seemed to be prattling facts. Like a talking textbook in *second silent scream* pleated-front khakis.

"Oh, we know!" Cheri nodded, attempting to defrost Albert with a warm smile. She searched deep in his eyes for some sort of reaction. For the boy who once kissed her underneath the schoolyard fluffula tree. But all she saw was the double reflection of her green data streams in his glasses. "We've got all that, Albert."

"Meaning what?" Opal said tersely. Something about Cheri's scatterbrained brilliance bugged Opal almost as much as Iris's purply perfectness.

"Meaning we're going to kick-start your zombos!" Scarlet had been struggling to stay still all this time and had only broken that one chair and maybe cracked a couple of cake platters all afternoon. But now she sprung up in a split scissor leap, bashing in a ceiling tile with her raised fist. When she dropped back down, she broke into a *boom-boom-clap, boom-boom-clap*, stomping her feet so hard she could have rocked an entire stadium. "We will, we will, re-shock you!" she sang—really projecting, too, like she'd learned in drama club rehearsals.

The zombos picked up the stomp. But what they sang sounded slightly different . . .

"We will, we will, stop you," they mumbled, shuffling forward like they do in that famous music video, except at least not all rotting and undead. And the way they said it, it sounded more like, "*Weevil, weevil, shamu.*" Which made Darth chitter with skunk snickers—it must have been an animal inside joke.

Still, the Ultra Violets knew what they meant.

The stamping and chanting got louder and louder, chairs rattling on the floor, balloons bouncing so vigorously that a few flew off the wall and floated into the crowd like beach balls at a concert. Then, apropos of totally nothing, the double doors from the diner burst open and everyone fell silent as . . .

. . . the saxophone-playing clown boogied in and started wailing out a super-cheesy jam.

"Let's go, girls!" Iris called just as Opal whipped both her arms around in wide circles, snapping her fingers at her minions. "Stop them!" she commanded.

And that is officially when the party went out of bounds.

Darth scampered up onto Cheri's shoulder as she reached into her tote bag and pulled out one end of . . . the string of holiday lights?

"Got it!" Scarlet called, grabbing the cord from Cheri's hand and spinning off in one direction. Cheri clicked down the wheels on her platform roller skates and, careful not to gum them up in the brussels sauce spill, went the other. Between them, they unraveled the holiday lights like a long rope. It wasn't easy to keep it from getting tangled. Every which way they turned, they stumbled into a stray chair or a table corner. Or a zombofied classmate.

"Ack!" Cheri squawked as a lumbering Brad, his eyes clouded over, clawed toward her. "*Mmnoh,*" he moaned. "*Dopes!*"

"Please, not the hair!" Cheri cried, slapping his hands back. On her shoulder, Darth turned around and, with a targeted squirt from his bling-ringed tail, shot out a stinky plume.

Bullziye! Darth thought.

"Burns!" Brad roared, stumbling backward.

On the other side of the room, Scarlet was fighting off the Jensen twins. They bared their matching buckteeth at her, chirping through the gaps like a couple of angry birds.

"You asked for it, sisters," Scarlet growled. "This is *my* angry face!" She arced a leg in *pointe tendu*, hooked both girls at the ankles, and flipped them off their feet. Out of nowhere, like it had been choreographed, two chairs slid Scarlet's way, and the twins each fell into a seat. Scarlet

scanned the room but saw nothing but zombos. With two swift kicks to the chairbacks, she sent the twins skidding toward the center of the room. Then she pirouetted-turned and elbowed zombo Ian in the gut just before he grabbed her.

"Oof!" he uttered, doubling over. She booted him toward the middle of the room, too.

Cheri was at one end, unwinding holiday lights, while Darth sprayed the funk on any zombotic student who came too close. Scarlet was at the other, corralling them behind her end of the line with *grands battements* and karate chops. Iris, after checking to see that all was underway with the hastily named Plan K, dashed over to the baddy bag table.

Her blazing ultraviolet eyes took in the vile baggies, all those nauseating yellow Mall of No Returns gift pouches packed with Opaline's mind-numbing "perfume." The idea of the kids in her class breathing it in just so that they could be colorless drones . . . Ugh, it disgusted her. Iris was an artist. She was all about color!

Hasta la never! she thought, twirling one of her purple ringlets. Then she closed her eyes for just a second or—

"Hey, Iris!"

Her eyes popped open again.

Balancing beside her on his hoverboard was Sebastian, hair falling into his eyes, baddy bag in his hand.

Boys Come and Go: The Sequel

IRIS POWERED DOWN LICKETY-SPLIT, EVEN THOUGH she needed her ultraviolet rays if she was to destroy the—

"Aftershave, huh?" Sebastian said, digging into the despicable yellow bag and fishing the fun-size sample out of it. "That's dope," he joked. "And is this party messed up or what?" He lifted the vial of greenish-gray liquid to the light. "Those psycho balloons. The flash mob with the stomping. And then that clown with the saxophone shows up out of nowhere? Crazy! It's like a performance art piece or something—a happening! You know?"

Iris did know about happenings—when you act out your art, whatever you want it to be, and you get other people to join in, too. Iris had even thought that, with Scarlet's awesome dance talents and Cheri's naturally glam personality, the Ultra Violets could stage some viomazing performance art of their own. Involving lollipops and lots and lots of glitter dust . . .

But Opal's birthday party of gloom was no performance. It stunk for real.

"Oh, it's definitely 'something,'" Iris said, forcing herself to smile. She grabbed Sebastian's hand, the hand holding the mini-bottle of L'eau d'Opes, and pulled him closer. "You're still wearing the friendship bracelet," she pretended to notice, stalling for time. "That's supersweet!"

Sebastian's face broke into a broad grin and he flipped his hair back. It immediately fell right into his eyes again. "Your hand is so warm," he said.

"Is it?" Iris stammered. Of course it was! Three seconds earlier and it would have been ultraviolet-hot! She wished she could evaporate the perfume right out of Sebastian's fingers, but she knew she couldn't do that without burning him, too. "I'm so surprised to see you!" she said instead. "What are you guys doing here, anyway?"

"Doug's cousin Ian told us about it," Sebastian explained. "And Malik remembered your friend mentioning a party that day behind the ice cream shop. I wanted to see you again . . ."

Iris's smile came easily this time. But she could hear the ruckus going on behind them. All she could think was that, at any second now, zombo Ian might break a plate over his unsuspecting cousin's head.

"Hey," Sebastian said, dropping his voice, "can I ask you? Are you, like, in a fight now with the birthday girl? Things were getting pretty intense between the two of you before."

Iris tried to act abashed, faking a sheepish grin. "We did kind of have a teensy tiff," she admitted. *About mind-control of the entire student body!* She hunched up her shoulders apologetically, as if the whole thing could just be shrugged off. "You know how it can get, school cliques . . ."

"Yeah, I hate that stuff, too," Sebastian agreed. "Live and let live, I say." He switched the vial to his other hand and laced fingers with her. "No way this perfume does all the things she said"—he shook his head in disbelief— "but maybe it smells good enough to get everyone to chill already." He jiggled the mini-bottle back and forth, and little brackish bits floated in the murk. "Plus, after that brussels sprout sauce," he teased, "this whole party needs a breath-freshener." Sebastian raised the moldy L'eau d'Opes sample spray, about to squirt some onto his tongue.

With a swift smack, Iris knocked it right out of his hand. It went sailing across the room and smashed into the wall, where it left a greasy black stain. Before Sebastian could even react, Iris whipped out a spare candy ring from her hoodie pocket and popped it into his mouth like a baby's pacifier.

"To go with the bracelet!" she said, blinking at him with her periwinkle eyes. "None out of five dentists says candy freshens breath *and* helps prevent cavities! Instead of that gunky green weirdness, okay? For me?"

Sebastian gazed into those pale blue pools, slightly shocked, wondering what had just happened. But then the taste of the blueberry candy—a little bit sweet, a little bit sour, a little bit tart, and definitely deep—brought the smile back to his face. He was reminded again that Iris always surprised him. She was certainly a strange girl. And there was something deep and wonderful about that, too.

"Okay, Iris," he murmured, lowering his head toward hers, talking with the candy ring between his teeth. "For you, I think I would do anything."

Eeek! Iris blushed violet, two heart-shaped spots blooming on her cheeks. OMV, how come every time she got with Sebastian there was always a mutant or a mob of zombotic kids or whatever to deal with?! But boys come and go. And her girls needed her! With all the self-control she could muster, she lifted her head slightly, and before their lips could touch, she pulled back just a bit and said, "Really? Anything?"

"For reals," Sebastian whispered in her ear.

Iris glanced over her shoulder. Cheri and Scarlet had some of the kids rounded up, but there were still plenty of stragglers pulverizing everything in their path. Opal was shooting electrical currents at Scarlet's superfast feet. BellaBritney was shaking her stubby pompom in Cheri's face.

Darth had squirted so much sweet violet stink into the eyes of zombos, the air was thick with his smog. Iris swallowed, wishing she didn't have to manipulate her crush like this. But she did.

"Then would you mind helping my friends get everyone together?" she asked. "For, um, a special surprise to end the party. The last performance art piece! You could be a part of it!"

"Okay, cool!" Sebastian replied with real enthusiasm—because he was an artist as well. "And then we can meet up after, just the two of us?"

"Definitely!" Iris said, a catch in her throat. For an instant she felt like she might cry. Sebastian was so nice, and it seemed like all she ever did was fool him. But for a good cause! To hide her tears, she flung her arms around his waist and gave him a tight squeeze as he wobbled on his hoverboard. "Thank you!" she mumbled, wiping her eyes on his T-shirt. "Thank you so much!"

Sebastian didn't notice how torn Iris was. Her hug only seemed to encourage him more. "No problem!" he practically crowed, the candy ring still clenched between his teeth. And he zoomed off toward the center of the room.

Iris took a deep breath. Dabbed her eyes with the sleeve of her ugly beige hoodie. And turned her attention back to the table of BeauTek baddy bags. She might not get another chance. In a blink, she turned up her heat again, until her fingertips throbbed and her eyes blazed. Glowering at the gift bags, aiming both hands at them, she scorched them to a crisp with a double blast of ultraviolet beams. Her fire burned so hot that the glass vials melted before they could burst, and all the chemicals in the perfume exploded into a mini mushroom cloud. Or maybe it looked more like a broccoli floret. The hideous yellow baggies, the BeauTek potion inside them, the creepy brackenish bits, the cheap plastic tablecloth: Within seconds, they had all disintegrated to a smoldering layer of charcoaled dust.

Iris dropped her temperature again, low enough that she wouldn't burn holes through everything she looked at, everything she touched. And then, for good measure, she took another breath and—*OhmV*—blew at the cinders.

They scattered off the table and into nothingness.

The score at halftime: L'eau d'Opes = up in smoke. Opaline and the zombos = still going strong. Sebastian and his hoverboarding buddies were helping with the roundup, herding strays behind the holiday-light line for what they hoped would be an awesome end-of-party performance. But Scarlet was dancing on her own, all the way on the other side of the room. She arched her feet in *relevé* and searched for the next zombotomized classmate. She could see Opal and Cheri fighting over Abby O'Adams, who had recovered from her fainting spell but still had tomato sauce on her face.

Scarlet knew she possessed superstrength and delivered precision pirouettes. But she was still a bit surprised at how smoothly her part of Operation Get-O had gone. She could hear plates and glasses shattering all around her, but never once did she get hit. If she needed a chair to knock some kid into, one would suddenly appear at her side. And it seemed like fresh zombotrons didn't stumble her way until she'd dealt with the ones before them. When they did reach her, some of them already had their hands tied behind their backs with ripped-up party streamers or knotted cloth napkins. Scarlet didn't get it. Cheri was roller-skating in the middle of the chaos, Darth riding on her shoulders. Iris was off obliterating the baddy bags. How could either one of them possibly have time to be helping her, too?

Scarlet *jetéed* onto a table, pressed down her tongue with two fingers, and whistled sharply across the room. Cheri glanced up from her tug-o'-Abby-O'Adams with Opal, and Scarlet flashed her the V sign. Then she jumped down again and dashed over to the retro jukebox. Sure enough, behind it was an electrical outlet with one socket free. Scarlet stretched the cord of holiday lights taut. Her long bangs brushed across her eyes, and she stuck out her lower lip in concentration, completely forgetting how Cheri's glittery gloss had felt so funny at first. She was just . . . about . . . there . . . when . . .

She felt something rapidly wrapping around her. Coiling around her thighs, then her hips, then her waist, then her arms. Tightening . . .

"Hey!" Scarlet cried out in alarm as she was lifted off the ground.

Gripping Scarlet with her scaly tail, her forked tongue flicking with smug satisfaction, was her old cafeteria nemesis Karyn Karson. The girl she'd once humiliated by ninja-kicking a bowl of ravioli on her head—but only to stop her from throwing them at Albert Feinstein. *And look where that got me!* Scarlet thought, struggling against the constricting lizard lock. Back then, Karyn was just a mean girl. But now she was a mutant. Which meant she was strong, too.

"Sssscarlet Louisssse Jonessss," Karyn sibilated, her reptile eyes narrowed to slits. "I alwaysss sssussspected it wasss you who dumped thhhat ravioli on me. But you know whhhen I figured it out for ssssure?"

"Don't know, don't care!" Scarlet shot back, trying to kick her in the stomach. With K-Liz's tail notched tight around her thighs, she could scarcely move her feet.

"It wasss at your audition for the ssschool play," Karyn seethed. "Whhhen I sssaw how hhhigh and how fffar and how fffasssssst you jumped."

"Or maybe Opal just told you!" Scarlet spat, wrestling to break free. She still gripped the cord of the holiday lights in her hand. But Karyn's tail squeezed around her shoulders. Scarlet wondered if this was what mummies felt like, or magicians in straitjackets. She wanted to scream out, for

Iris, for Cheri. But Karyn had her bound so tight, she could barely breathe. "And you deserved it!" Scarlet gasped. "You were catapulting ravioli at Albert! Now you and Two-Face and Opal have rewired his brain!" Panting, she added, "Can't you get friends any other way than by being a bully?"

At this Karyn just laughed, and as her *ha-ha-ha*s slid past her forked tongue, they just came out as hisses. "The more you ssstruggle," she said, that split tongue tip licking at Scarlet's ear, "the tighhhter I ssssqueeze."

Scarlet rocked her shoulders and flailed her feet. She held her breath and pushed out so hard she thought the freckles might pop off her cheeks. Karyn just ha-ha-hissed all the more, enjoying her pain.

This is it! Scarlet despaired. *I'm gonna die at Opal's insane birthday party, crushed by a mutant lizard girl while a clown plays the saxophone! I'll never get to be Little Orphan Annie! I'll never get to dance again!*

This last realization was too much to bear. Never to pas de deux or tango or paso doble, to flamenco or fandango or bhangra, never to feel that movement, that glorious freedom. Ever!

No.

It couldn't be over.

Oh swell no!

Not yet.

There was still one part of Scarlet's body that K-Liz hadn't wrapped her tail around.

"This," Scarlet growled through gritted teeth, "is gonna hurt me. But it's gonna hurt you more!"

Like a bucking bronco, her aubergine ponytail swishing behind her, Scarlet reared back, ready to deliver a superpowered head-butt that would surely knock her unconscious, too. But just as her forehead made contact with K-Liz's scaly brow, the mutant let out an ear-piercing ssscreech and her tail lost all its tension. Scarlet tumbled to the floor. K-Liz's butchered tail dropped down with her.

"Gah!" Scarlet screamed. She tried to scooch away but couldn't move, all the feeling gone from her body. The chopped-off tail flopped beside her like a fish out of water. Above her, Karyn spun in circles, clutching at the stump where it had been. And standing a step behind, cake knife in hand, was Agent Jack Baxter.

"You!" Scarlet gasped, propping herself up on her knees, her legs still numb. "You were the one helping me all along!"

Agent Jack's chest rose and fell beneath his black suit jacket. But he said nothing.

"I totally had that, you know," Scarlet stated, shakily getting to her feet as a still-shrieking Karyn slithered away. "I was just about to—"

"Head-butt her to infinity and beyond," Agent Jack said, offering her his arm. "Yeah, I saw. And yeah, I know. You're a rock star, Scarlet Jones. You're a supergirl. You don't need some *lil'* boy's help. So don't even say it."

"Fine, I won't." Scarlet managed a trembly shrug, trying to sound nonchalant. But she did grip Jack's arm as if it were a ballet barre, to steady herself. And something about what he'd said made her feel just as trembly inside.

They stood there for a moment, each eyeing the other warily. The chaos of the roundup crashed on behind them. "Why did you do it?" Scarlet asked at last, in a softened voice, as one of Opal's stray lightning bolts streaked high above their heads. "You're on their side. You're a spy for BeauTek."

At this Agent Jack just breathed out heavily and shook his head. Scarlet could see that there must have been much he wanted to say. But he kept it all inside. "Guess I'm curious to see your big stage debut," he answered, dodging the question. "How many *Lil'* Orphan Annies have black belts in taekwondo?"

Scarlet felt herself starting to smile. To stop it, she gave herself a weak thump on the shoulder. But it was no use. She kept smiling anyway.

"That, um, purple glitter stuff," Agent Jack mumbled. "On your. Face. Looks . . . good."

"Thanks," Scarlet said, embarrassed. She realized she was still holding his arm. "Hey, I think you might have grown an inch! Since that last time I saw you. After the, um, poker game," she babbled, even more embarrassed as she recalled her swirlie threats.

"Affirmatively?" Jack said, surprised. And finally he allowed himself the lil'est of smiles, too. Though he quickly grew serious again. "Are you going to take me down now, with all these zombos?" he asked. "Because I work for BeauTek?"

"I probably should . . ." Scarlet searched his face, waiting to see if he'd ask her not to. But she couldn't quite read his expression.

"Probably," was all he said.

"But—" It was hard for Scarlet to admit this next part. Sometimes the truth hurts. "You did just sort of save my life."

"You're welcome," Agent Jack answered, figuring that was as close to a thank you as he was going to get. He cleared his throat. "So I guess you have a 'single awesome solar event' to do . . ."

"OMV!" Scarlet realized, the light cord still clasped tightly in her hand. She let go of Jack's arm and *grand-pliéed* down, reached behind the jukebox in *arabesque*, then plugged it in. Rainbow colors twinkled all the way across the room.

And when Scarlet *pliéed* back up, Agent Jack was once again gone.

28

Solar Awesomeness

HOW VERY THOUGHTFUL OF THE ULTRA VIOLETS TO decorate Opaline's brainwashing party with holiday lights! Ha ha, no, not really. Although a string of pretty bling certainly couldn't hurt, because things had gotten *très* ugly there in Tom's Diner.

And Opaline's twelfth birthday wasn't over yet.

Like Superman's kid sister, Scarlet bounced over to Cheri and Iris in a single bound. Immediately the girls began winding the other end of the holiday lights around each of the zombotomized students clustered together in the sticky brussels sprout puddle: Rachel and Abby; Martin and Brad; Julie and the Jensen twins; and, of course, Albert. Whenever Opal or BellaBritney tried to stop them, Cheri wheeled around on her platform roller skates and—oh how the odors had turned!—Darth squirted them with a sickening perfume of his own.

Considering that not five minutes before, Scarlet herself had been wrapped up in a lizard tail, it was a curious flip-flop of events. Being bound by a lizard tail had been hideous. At least the holiday lights were pretty. Yet the question remained: What strange party game were the Ultra Violets playing?

Indeed, just as they abhorred beige, the Ultra Violets adored bright colors. Few things were more merry and bright than holiday lights—maybe a rainbow, but that's it. Tying up the zombos with such a cheerful string could have been a way to make them happier again.

But that's not why the Ultra Violets did it.

The holiday lights were rigged. By them. Each tiny bulb had been cracked open and its wires exposed. By them! As Cher and Scar and RiRi loop-de-looped and do-si-doed around the corralled kids, they hooked each one up to a light. Some got connected at their braces. Some got attached at their earrings. Still others at their nose studs. And for those students who had neither metal piercings nor braces? The girls had no choice but to paper-clip a light directly onto their earlobe.

Yes, the rejiggered string of holiday lights was, in fact, a homemade . . . well, Albert put it best, announcing it to the whole room as a festive orange bulb blinked from his braces.

"It is a multi-clamp jumper cable," he rattled off, still in robotone.

Cheri *tsk-tsk*ed at the sight of him. Hooking a holiday light to Albert's braces had done nothing to improve his pleated pants situation. "We're not going to win any decorating awards with this mess!" she said, surveying the twinkling mob.

Iris was just taking her tablet out of her messenger bag. "Think of it as modern art instead," she said, smiling over her shoulder at Sebastian. He and his buds had hovered off to the back wall, waiting to see just what this final performance piece was going to be.

Scarlet patched the other end of the cord into Iris's computer while Cheri clicked open the program they'd created. "Just don't hit me, okay?" Scarlet said. "'Cause by now I probably sweated off all my sunscreen."

"No worries!" Iris promised, powering up again. "My aim is a lot better than it used to be."

"Hurry, guys," Cheri urged, casting a worried glance at Opal, who was going from table to table splashing glasses of water into her face to rinse her stinging eyes of Darth's stench. "Those lights won't hold the class for long!" From his hiding spot back inside the tote bag, Darth nudged up her cat-eye sunglasses. Cheri passed them to Scarlet.

"Then let's get this party ended," Scarlet declared, looking more like a rock star than ever in Cheri's black shades. She flipped the tablet over and held it above her head, old-school boom-box style. The back, not the screen, faced Iris. The back of her solar-powered, solar-paneled computer. "Fire away!" Scarlet cried.

"And remember," Cheri whispered to Iris. She couldn't look directly at her anymore because she was already beaming. "For the mass transient variation of current, hit the solar panels with extreme ultraviolet C-level radiation—in the range of about a hundred nanometer rays."

"Um, okay, Cher," Iris said nervously.

She actually hadn't the slightest clue how to measure that. To Iris, extreme ultraviolet was just the opposite of beige. The best she could do, she figured, was shine diamond-bright.

Iris bore down on the solar panels, drilling two blistering, near-invisible, violet light beams at them with her eyes. She raised both hands and pointed both pinkies and shot laser-thin UV rays. The panels soaked up the tremendous influx of solar energy. Sent it from the tablet computer out through the cord. And it coursed into all the holiday lights clamped to the zombo class. The currents began to crackle back into their brains, reactivating the nerve centers Opal had numbed with her signature scent. Some kids began to jerk spasmodically, sparking and blinking wherever the light was attached to their head. Slowly, some of them started to smile.

"It's working!" Cheri shouted, her mind racing with ratios. "Iris, turn it up three more degrees and your solar power surge will override Opal's shutdown!"

Iris didn't answer. She couldn't. Every ounce of her attention, every drop of her energy, was pouring out of her. If only she could burn a little brighter . . .

"Stop! Stop it stop it stop it!" Opal's command ricocheted across the room, backed up by a ridiculous cheer of "S-T-O-P Stop!"

Iris didn't stop. She wasn't even sure where Opal was, and she didn't dare turn her head to look—she'd burn everything in her sight line. But through the screen of Cher's black sunglasses, Scarlet spotted their ex-bestie.

"Ruh-roh," she muttered.

While BellaBritney idiotically kicked up one leg beside her, Opal strained to channel her own electricity. With one pinkie rubber-topped by the purple polymer, her powers were hampered. But she still had her other hand.

Opal focused just as hard as Iris, white fog cloaking her eyes. As she did, a coal-black rain cloud curled beneath the ceiling. It roiled and boomed over Iris's blinding sunbeams, their heat burning off the condensation before it could rain.

Rolling together electric currents like cookie dough, Opal formed a ball of lightning in the palm of her hand.

"Iris, watch out!" Scarlet cried.

But Iris couldn't move. *If I lose power now*, she realized, *I'll never be able to build it up again. Not high enough. Not in time.*

Opal hauled back and threw the first pitch. The awkwardness of the pinkie cap made the toss clumsy. It grazed Iris across the back of her thighs, the razor edges of the spinning lightning bolts slicing straight lines in her beige trackpants before exploding into the wall.

"Owie," Iris gasped, hoping she was not now flashing her purple panties at Sebastian and his friends. *Then I would be a sun AND a moon*, it occurred to her. And she wondered how she could possibly be thinking up jokes in the middle of a superhero showdown.

Cheri stood by helplessly as Opal began to shape her next lightning-bolt ball. *Darth, what can we do?* she thought, chewing her thumbnail in spite of herself. *If Opal keeps chucking lightning balls at Iris, sooner or later she's going to make contact!*

From his hiding spot inside the tote bag, Darth answered, *We needz bazeball bat.*

"But there are no baseball bats in diners!" Cheri cried aloud.

Watching the "performance art" from the back of the room, Malik applauded her dramatic outburst—which must have meant something very profound. Even Goth Bella paused to give her props, because it sounded like her kind of poem. Cheri ignored them both. Instead, her glowing infra-green eyes scanned the party room, registering the spatial dimensions of every item in sight. The place was a total disaster zone. Off in one corner she could see the blackened spot where the BeauTek gift bags had been obliterated. Tables were upside down, chairs flipped on their sides, the floor covered with shattered plates and shards of glass, forks and knives and spoons, all of it stuck in dried-up brussels sprout sauce. The whole scene offended Cheri's delicate sensibilities! And just as she feared, there was not a baseball bat to be found.

But then her eyes fell upon something else . . .

"Shine on, RiRi!" she called, skating off. "I'll be right back!"

Be right back?! Iris thought. *But where is Cher going?!*

Another of Opal's lightning balls crackled past, this one lobbed too high. It rocketed above Iris's head, over the slowly recharging zombos, and crashed into the top row of scary smileys. Five balloons burst at once, the toxic perfume inside them sizzling into the ether. Their *pops!* couldn't even be heard over the rumble of thunder.

Scarlet's arms were *not* getting tired holding up the solar tablet. *No! They're! Not!* she commanded herself. Sweat dripped down her face, plastering her long bangs against her forehead. Since Opal's psycho party had begun, Scarlet must have tackled and tied up twenty zombos. Then there was the squeeze-off with a mutant. *But I! Am not! Tired!* she shouted inside.

And all of a sudden she realized why Agent Jack always talked like that. It was very motivating. In a boot camp kind of way.

The sight of one of Opal's lightning balls zooming toward her sharpened her focus. Instinctively Scarlet hopped to the side in *petit allegro*—she had to! To keep from being knocked over like a bowling pin! In that split second, Iris's solar beams shot straight ahead, smoking a big hole right in the middle of poster-girl Opal and burning away another batch of the poisonous balloons.

"Sorry, RiRi!" Scarlet called, hopping back into position. She couldn't look behind her to see what was up with the zombos. But she thought she heard groaning . . .

They're starting to loosen the cord, Iris panicked, staring right at them. *They're going to break free before we can reboot them!* She was blazing as hard as she could, but she knew she couldn't keep it up forever. Soon she would be drained of energy. Empty. She felt like she might faint. If she did, would a mob of her own classmates stampede right over her?

Opaline sensed Iris weakening. She snickered, whipping up her biggest lightning ball yet. "Gimme a one! Gimme a two! Gimme a strike three!" BellaBritney cheered her on with her shorn pompom, both of her personalities excited by the chaos. Opal wound up for the death pitch, spitting, "O na na! What's my name?" Then she leaned back. And released a split-finger fastball. Headed straight for Iris's heart.

Iris couldn't see the pitch—she couldn't turn away. But she could feel it coming. She could hear the fizz of the balled-up, barbed-wired lightning bolts as they cut through the air. She could imagine the shock, like a hundred electric knife blades stabbing her at once. It would blast her right off her feet. It would finish her on the spot.

SHAZAM IT! she screamed inside, reaching deep, detonating more energy than she even knew she had. She felt her hair stand on end. She rocked back as the awesome solar surge burst out of her. And she'd done it! She knew she'd done it! She thought she'd done it? She hoped she had, desperately. It was better than the best she could give. It was the ultimate. It was the ultra. She'd done it, and she was done. It didn't matter now whether Opal's jagged lightning ball hit her. Whether it completely blew her away . . .

And here it comes, Iris thought, starting to faint, starting to fall. The snakelike hiss of the approaching electricity was so close, itching at her ear. And then . . .

BLAMMO!

Cheri stepped right into the line of fire. Stepped in swinging. Swinging at that lightning death pitch, swinging for the ceiling. But no, not with a baseball bat. There are no baseball bats in diners.

With a saxophone.

Cheri caught the lightning ball in the gaping bell of the horn. Then she spun around on her platform skates and whipped it right out again. Scarlet's mouth dropped open as she saw it barreling toward her, a high-voltage bomb. Suddenly she realized what Cheri had done. And she turned to face it head on.

KA-POW! Opal's lightning ball, hooked by a saxophone and then hurled out again, exploded into the computer panels right after Iris's awesome burst. The combination of the solar power and the electrical energy surged through the holiday lights, shocking all the kids off the ground—and back

to their senses. It was a magnificent explosion. Sunbeams burst out of ears and mouths. Rainbow-colored lights rained down like fireworks. All the scary smiley balloons combusted. And all the recharged kids jumped to their feet, tearing off the blown-out lightbulbs they found clamped to their faces. They began talking excitedly, wondering what had just happened. And why three hoverboys were giving them a standing ovation.

Scarlet dropped the fried tablet and rushed over to Iris, who had collapsed onto the floor.

"Iris!" Cheri whispered, already by her side. "We did it!"

"We kick-started all our friends!" Scarlet said, giving her a shake.

Iris didn't reply. She just lay there, motionless, while Darth tickled her nose with his tail, which he'd scented lightly of smelling salts.

"Water, now!" Scarlet cried out, alarmed. She looked up into the gathering crowd, only to see a full glass right beside her, as if it had been there before she'd even asked. *Thanks again, Jack*, she thought. She was too worried to smile.

Sebastian had zoomed up and hopped off his hoverboard. He knelt down next to Iris and gently put an arm beneath her shoulders. "She's got a super-high temperature!" he announced, feeling her forehead. Cheri and Scarlet exchanged knowing glances. Then Scarlet held the glass of water up to her mouth, trying to get her to drink.

Iris moaned lightly. Her eyelids fluttered, tiny flickers of pale violet light flashing between her lashes. When she blinked them open, the first thing she saw was Sebastian's face, his lips pursed with worry, gazing down at her. She smiled feebly as he said, "Iris, that was AWESOME! How did you do it? You are *so* committed to your art!"

Iris was too wiped out to come up with another lie. But she didn't have to. Before she could even take a breath to speak, she was interrupted by one seriously unhappy birthday girl.

"Ugh, spare me!"

Opaline stood on the edge of the circle, shooting daggers at the three girls. (Not literally, at least not this time. That's just another way of saying she was giving them the major stink eye. Also not literally, since all her poisonous perfume had been evaporated. The point is, she was irked to the max.) "I hope you're all happy now," she began.

"We are!" the rebooted guests shouted with glee.

Opal stamped her foot in fury. Then she bowed down over the Ultras, her eyes still streaming with clouds, her hair frazzled and frizzy, the ends of her patent yellow Peter Pan collar curled up from all the crazy weather. "You three may have ruined my birthday party," she sneered. "But you haven't smelled the last of me yet!"

And with quick, hard yanks, Opaline pulled their hair. One, two, three: Iris, Scarlet, Cheri.

"Owie!" Cher yelped, covering her head as Opaline ran out the swinging doors.

The beehived waitress strutted in right after her. She took one look at the destruction and her eyebrows shot up into her bouffant. She marched right over to the kids. Then marched right past them.

Without uttering a single word, the waitress gave the jukebox a hefty hip bump. As she sashayed out of the party room again, the music began to play.

"Ooh, I love this song!" Cheri clapped, forgetting about her hair.

"Me too!" Scarlet shouted, leaping to her feet. "Let's dance!"

And there among the ruins, with Iris still lying on the floor, her head in Sebastian's lap, that's exactly what everybody did.

29

Return of the
Mall of No Returns

LATER THAT EVENING . . .

. . . across the Joan River . . .

. . . inside an acid-yellow abandoned shopping mall . . .

. . . up two flights of escalators on lonely level C . . .

. . . locked behind the two glossy pink doors of the top-secret Vi-Shush lab . . .

. . . a twelve-year-old girl and her mother were performing a postmortem. An autopsy, as it were. Dissecting the details of a spectacularly disastrous birthday party.

"Oh honey," Dr. Trudeau said, dipping Opaline's pinkie finger in a special solvent that would dissolve the purple polymer cap—in another eight hours or so. "I know you're disappointed."

"Shut up, Mom," Opal groused. The words came out in a mush, her cheek squishing her mouth sideways as she propped up her chin in her other hand.

"Don't say 'shut up,' Opaline," Dr. Trudeau scolded. "It's not polite. The important thing is that you tried."

"No it's not!" Opal snapped. "And whoever says that is a liar! The important thing is that *we* failed!"

"Failure is a vital part of the scientific process, sweetie," Dr. Trudeau said, using her soothingest voice. "Everyone here at BeauTek knows that. It's the sixth point in the company's mission statement. That I drafted."

Opal rolled her eyes. Her mother was forever drafting contracts and clauses and press releases as part of her job at BeauTek. As far as Opal was concerned, it was all just a bunch of mumbo jumbo that adults came up with to cover their butts.

"We'll find another test group to roll out our trial run of L'eau d'Opes," her mother continued. "Don't you worry your electric little head about it. In fact, Sir Develon is spearheading a plan to broaden the base. Why just enslave your classmates when we've got an entire city of oblivious citizens at our disposal? Right across the river."

A surly Opal swirled her purple pinkie in the liquid solvent. She'd only encountered Develon Louder, the president of BeauTek, on a couple of occasions. But they'd been enough to convince Opal that the woman was bat-poop bonkers. She talked at you from behind a giant black pocketbook. No, actually, she *shouted* at you from behind a giant black pocketbook. Every other word was a curse.

And she made all her employees call her "sir." What was *that* about? Then again, the woman had built BeauTek from the ground up. Bat-poop bonkers or not, she had a way of getting what she wanted. And if what she wanted was complete control of Sync City, well, Opal wanted that, too.

"What about those boys you mentioned?" she said, changing the subject. "The spies. What happened to them?"

"Hmm, that's another story," Dr. Trudeau replied, rolling *her* eyes. "One of them is on board, but he reminds me of a chlorofluorocarbon. Or the acetone in this solvent."

She paused, waiting for Opaline to get the joke. Her daughter just stared at her blankly.

"That means he's a *volatile* organic compound," her mother explained. "Get it? His temper could land him in trouble." She tittered at her own wit.

Opaline just shook her head. She was in no mood for nerdy scientist humor. "And the other one?" she asked.

"The other one," Dr. Trudeau answered, turning serious again, "I suspect might be a double agent."

"A double agent!" Opal whined, pulling her hand out of the solvent and pounding the stainless steel tabletop. "You mean he's secretly working for the Ultra Violets?! Great!" Opal stuck her pinkie finger back into the solvent so forcefully that it splashed up the sides of the bowl. "Could this birthday *be* any worse?"

"Now now, I don't know for sure," Dr. Trudeau said,

flinching as drops of watery purple solvent splashed onto her clean white lab coat. "But I've got that boy signed to a *very* strict contract—"

"I bet you do," Opal grumbled, and the two fell silent. For a few minutes the only sounds to be heard were the percolating of beakers and the pitter-patter of squeakers as lab mice ran on the wheels in their cages.

"That stupid FLab is so stupid," Opal said at last, repeatedly.

"I know, sweetie. I used to work there, remember?" Dr. Trudeau reached out and tentatively began to comb the knots from her daughter's tangled bob.

"How can anyone take them seriously with a name like 'FLab'?" Opal complained, wincing each time the comb snagged. "It's ludicrous!"

"It certainly is," Dr. Trudeau agreed, trying to calm her down.

"Mommy?" Opal asked, suddenly feeling very tired.

"Yes, sweetie?" Dr. Trudeau answered, brushing the back of Opal's head smooth and straight again.

"Promise me that BeauTek will keep breaking into the FLab? Please? Pinkie-swear that we'll find a way to stop the Ultra Violets. Stop them from being so . . . so . . ." Opal flipped through her mental dictionary, searching for any other word. But only one would do. "So *ultra*," she said at last, with a defeated sigh.

"I don't even have to promise, honey," Dr. Trudeau

responded with confidence. "And I don't think pinkie swears are legally binding. But I already have it in writing. Option seventeen of the corporate espionage clause."

Opaline laid her head down. With her free pinkie, she toyed with three colorful strands on the stainless steel tabletop.

"There's my supertrouper," Dr. Trudeau said, patting Opal on her back. "Though we'd better put those away now."

"But they're so pretty," Opaline puled. "They're the best thing I got for my birthday."

"You can play with them later," her mother said, plucking them up between the fingers of her latex-gloved hands and plopping each one into its own plastic evidence pouch. "These belong in the files, along with all the other evidence we collect."

"I know," Opal agreed reluctantly.

"Now, tell me again," Dr. Trudeau said, taking out a marker and labeling each bag.

"The berry-red one is Cheri Henderson," Opal recited.

"Indeed," said Dr. Trudeau, writing it down. "Gilder of the lily . . ." she added under her breath. "And the licorice-black belongs to that rambunctious Scarlet Jones. And—"

"And the prettiest pretty purple one is Iris Tyler," Opal murmured, as if in a dream.

"Excellent!" her mother exclaimed, snapping the cap back on the marker. "Why don't you get some rest, Opaline?" she suggested, standing up from the lab table. "I'll just nip over to the food court and nab you a peach soda."

"And maybe a piece of chocolate cake, too?" Opal asked. "From the automat?"

"We'll have our own special birthday celebration," Dr. Trudeau said, giving Opal's shoulders a squeeze. "Just you and me, right here in the Vi-Shush."

"And then tomorrow we'll look at those blueprints?" Opal asked, beginning to feel a bit better. "And the plans for the river?"

Right as she said it, the entire mall shook with a sonic *BOOM!* that gurgled up from far below them. Six levels under, to be exact, in the sub-sub-parking lot.

"Hear that, honey?" Dr. Trudeau beamed. "It's the sound of your future, Opaline. Of our future. Of BeauTek's future! Booming!"

Opal's eyes were closed, her cheek pressed against the cool lab table. The stainless steel reflected a small smile.

"It's a brand-new year for you, sweetie!" her mother chimed. "The big 1-2!" Before she dashed out the double pink doors, she called back, "Keep feeling fascination!"—forgetting that Fascination was precisely what the *F* in FLab stood for.

"Mwah-kay, Mommy," Opal mumbled drowsily. "Mwah-ha-kay. Mwah-ha-mwah-ha-ha . . ."

And she drifted off into the most delightful nightmare.

Get Out!

DEAREST READERS, COOL GIRLS AND FAN BOYS, BOOKISH cats and dogs, loyal devotees of the Ultra Violets: As this second story in their superheroic saga draws to a close, what have we learned?

Not much, I hope! That's what school is for. Although if *erstwhile* ever pops up on a vocabulary quiz, I, Sophie Bell, your plus-size personal flight attendant on this purple-empowered magic carpet ride, will privately weep glitterdust tears if you do not know the definition!

Forgive me. I get so emotional when it comes to *sniff* goodbyes. Parting being such sweet sorrow, etc. *dabs eyes with feather boa* And O to the MV, what a long, strange trip it's been.

The good news? The Ultra Violets foiled Opaline's plot to reprogram their Chronic Prep class into Debbie Downers and Crabby Patties, Gloomy Georges and Melancholy Melvins, Sullen Samanthas and Woebegone Joes. Let's not forget the

Bummed-Out Howards, either. Bummed-Out Howards are the worst! Completely unbearable, take it from me: You do *not* want a Bummed-Out Howard on your hands. If you spot a Bummed-Out Howard headed your way, turn around and run in the opposite direction. Screaming optional. (*Like this, at the top of your lungs: "Optional! Gah! Optional! Ack!"*)

Awesome that the UVs put a stop to all that sadness and rebooted the student body with a massive surge of solar power—topped by one of Opaline's very own lightning balls, like the cherry bomb on a dynamite sundae. That was pretty genius of the girls, to use Opal's own evil energy against her. Even if they do now owe some clown a new saxophone.

So much for the awesome. Moving on to the downright terrifying: BeauTek's blueprints for what-the-wha? And just who's going *BOOM!* in that sub-sub-parking lot? Don't ask me, I don't know, either!

But if there's even the skinniest, slimmiest shimmer of a silver lining to this latest black cloud Opaline is brewing, it's that another viomazing adventure can't be far away.

And speaking of clouds . . .

Candace had parked the cloudship on the roof of Club Very UV and left it idling. Recycled mist surrounded it, and its millions of tiny mirrors twinkled beneath the brume. Down in the club, Candace was crouched on the floor in front of the massive flower window, repairing a rusted old searchlight she'd flown over from the FLab. Official FLab toolbox by her side, she tinkered with the lamp while the girls filled her in on the birthday party fallout. Minus the blueprints and the sub-sub-parking-lot parts. Which they didn't even know about.

(*But you do.*)

"Whoa, girls, that sounds epic," Candace said, testing the light switch. "And the brussels sprout sauce sounds *barf*! Iris, are you all right now?"

Iris sat sideways in the fuzzy orange egg chair, contemplating a lollipop. Her long purple ringlets spiraled down one of the curved armrests, and her legs dangled over the other. Darth had scampered up into her lap. She ran her fingers over his violet-striped tail, lost in her thoughts.

"No worries," she said softly. "I'm all recharged now."

"Good," Candace said. Somehow she had smeared grease on her chin while fixing the lamp. It looked like an inky black goatee to go with her baby blond bangs. "It's major that you stopped BeauTek from turning Chronic Prep's sixth-grade class into a bunch of zombos—you girls rock. First mutants, then mind-control: Who knows what they'll whip up next at the Vi-Shush!"

Just the mention of that horrible laboratory gave Cheri the heebie-cheribies. From her spot on the marshmallow sofa, she shuddered and her hand slipped. By accident she daubed a dot of sparkling burgundy nail polish on the white cushions. It didn't look bad.

"So you don't think this is over yet?" she asked, even though she already knew the answer.

"Opaline is madder at us than ever," Scarlet said, in between upside-down jumping jacks. Dress rehearsals for the school play began next week, so she had even more nervous energy to burn than usual. "I really don't see how we could ever be friends again, Candace."

Candace didn't say anything. She just stuck the tip of her tongue out in concentration as she tightened a screw on the searchlight with a pointed prong of one of her trusty sporks. Scarlet was right: As long as Opal stayed evil, the Ultra Violets would have to keep fighting her. *Erstwhile* besties or not.

"There's something else," Iris said, swinging her feet down. She put Darth on the floor, and he scampered over to his potpourri pillow at Skeletony's feet to snuggle in for a skunk nap. Then she attempted a few wobbly pirouettes of her own, spinning over to the massive flower window to watch what Candace was doing.

"Hmm?" Candace murmured, attempting to swivel the searchlight up and down on its rusty axle. It stuck in spots, so she took an eyedropper out of her toolbox and squeezed a few greasy beads into the joints of the machine. "Baby oil," she stated. "Always does the trick. What were you saying, Iris?"

"It's just . . ." Iris paused, tugging on the end of one of her purple tendrils. She looked out the window, over to the rock-crystal FLab atop the Highly Questionable Tower glinting in the distance, then at the gleaming gold and silver spires of the Sync City skyline. She looked back into the clubhouse, at Scarlet and Cheri. "Guys, I'm pretty sure pretty much everyone saw us using our superpowers at Opal's party. Maybe they don't know what they saw. But they saw something."

Cheri daintily cleared her throat. "It's mostly you, RiRi," she said, in the gentlest way she could. "Alas. You're the one who glows violet and shoots off rainbows. I mean, it looks cosmically gorge when you do, but . . ."

"But it's not beige." Iris blushed, embarrassed. "I know. Cher, your eyes go into neon green data streams now, when you're supercomputing. Your hair turns magenta pink. Scarlet's changes to aubergine."

By now Scarlet was right side up again, her everyday-black ponytail swishing back and forth as she practiced cha-cha slides. "Hey, I can keep my superdancing on the downlow!" she protested. "Piece of cake."

"Maybe," Iris said, seriously doubting it, "but how can we explain why a, um, cute little pipsqueak like you is as strong as the Hulk?"

"I eat my Wheaties?" Scarlet offered weakly. She knew Iris had a point. Also, she never ate her Wheaties. They gave her a stomachache.

"Opaline knows about us, obvi," Iris stated. "Her mom knows, too."

"And the Black Swans," Cheri said, blowing on her hands to dry the polish. "At least the short, silent, salt-and-peppery one does," she added, narrowing her eyes at Scarlet.

Scarlet wrinkled her nose. She knew Cher was trying to tease some kind of gushy mushy reaction out of her, but she refused to take the bait. She still wasn't sure what to think about Agent Jack, and she wasn't about to beam her confusion all over the place like Iris and her spontaneous rainbows! That just wasn't Scarlet's style. But she hadn't forgotten how Agent Jack had called her a supergirl. Right to her face! "So what are we saying?" she asked, dropping the topic of the Black Swans.

Candace squirted some baby oil into the palm of her hand, rubbed it in, then used it to smooth down her flyaways. As she went to push herself up off the floor, her greasy fingers slipped and she flailed back like a beginning ice skater.

"What I think we're all thinking," she said when she was finally on her feet, "is that even though No One Must Know, some people already do."

"So maybe we don't deny it anymore." Iris tried to read the reactions on Cheri's and Scarlet's faces. "Maybe it's PDH all the way."

"PDH?" Cheri repeated, puzzled. She got up from the marshmallow couch and gave Darth a pat on the head, careful not to get fur in her fresh manicure. Then she rolled around the shag rug on her platforms to join Candace and Iris at the window. "What does PDH stand for?"

"Public Displays of Heroism," Iris explained.

"You mean we should come out as superheroes?" Scarlet said, astonished. "Take the purple to the people?" She raced forward in flying *brisé* ballerina steps.

"It's who we are." As Iris spoke, the setting sun behind her cast a hazy lavender halo around her curls. "It's who we're meant to be!" she declared. "Our destiny! We can't hide it. We never could, even when we tried to. Instead we should be, you know . . . out loud and proud!"

"Ultraviolet Pride!" Scarlet shouted, inspired. "Power to the Purple!" She bounced up to touch the ceiling, just because she could. If the ceiling hadn't been there, she might have bounced right up to the moon.

"The cat *is* kind of out of the bag already . . ." Cheri mused. Darth popped up his head at the mention. *Not here in the club,* Cheri thought to him. *No cats, don't worry!* He settled back down again.

"Right on, girls," Candace agreed, taking a step back to scrutinize the searchlight. She didn't seem surprised in the least by Iris's PDH suggestion. "With all the break-ins at the FLab . . . something's up. I don't know what. But we've got to be prepared. Next time it might not be just your class at Chronic Prep that needs you. It might be all of Sync City!"

"Eek," Cheri squeaked, slightly stressed by the idea.

"Whoot!" Scarlet whooped at the same time, kickboxing and karate-chopping the air.

All four of them stared out the flower window, across the Joan River to the nauseating yellow fortress of the Mall of No Returns. As they watched, a sonic boom exploded from the building. It was so loud it scared all the ombré otters out of the lipsticked reeds lining the banks and sent the nesting gingham geese in flight. A second boom followed, and the smokestacks behind the mall spewed brackenish black fumes shaped like broccoli florets.

"Ew." Cheri automatically went to hold her tote bag

close, even though she'd left it back by the sofa and she knew Darth was safe and sound on his pillow.

"They are definitely not just baking cookies over at BeauTek," Scarlet quipped.

"Opal did say we hadn't smelled the last of her." Iris folded her arms and lifted her chin, determined. "So what do we do now? What do we do next?"

"Right-this-minute now?" Candace spun a spork in each hand, then tucked them into her tool belt like a policewoman holstering her pistols. "We celebrate! You girls just had a viomazing victory! Triple High Fives! And in the meantime, I've been working on a project for the mayor. Iris, did you do that painting I texted you about?"

"The one on plastic?" Iris turned away from the belching BeauTek buildings and dashed over to the club's marble table to grab it. "Here it is."

"Compelling!" Candace raved, admiring it. "Delicate, yet powerful!" She bent down and slipped the sheet over the lens of the searchlight. A flick of a latch locked the painting in place. "How about a sneak preview?" she asked, flashing the girls a grin.

Then she flipped the switch.

A bright violet flower blossom beamed out from Club Very UV up into the twilight sky. It sparkled above the city, a symbol: a way to let the citizens know that everything would be all right. That the Ultra Violets were on the case!

"Cool," Scarlet cooed, then darted off to the beanbag.

"Pretty!" Cheri gasped.

"Purple!" Iris smiled.

"Watch out, evil-doers!" Scarlet called, returning to the group with her Super Soaker in hand. She shot off a big burst of glitter. "We are the Ultra Violets!"

"Ultra Violets Forever!" Cheri cheered.

"Ultra Violets for Life!" Iris cried.

As the sun set over Sync City and the flower power signal shone high above, the super trio stood in silhouette. For just a second or three, they linked pinkie fingers, and an ultraviolet wave pulsed around them, lighting up their hair pink, purple, aubergine. Then Cheri flared her perfectly manicured hands out to one side. Scarlet aimed her Super Soaker to the other. And in the middle, Iris raised her fist high. The glitter from the gun blast floated back down, dusting each of them with tiny pieces that glimmered in the shadow of the searchlight. The three best friends wondered what would happen next. And felt seriously ready for it.

"Bring it on!" Scarlet announced to the world.

"Bling it on!" Cheri giggled, shaking the glitter from her hair.

"Bring it in!" Iris said. And even Candace joined them for a supergroup hug.

Then they broke apart. And because they were really hungry, they ordered a pizza.

Beaucoup Gracias
{Acknowledgments}

SWATHED IN A PSYCHEDELIC TURQUOISE MUUMUU THAT serendipitously dropped from the sky, squaring her padded shoulders to confront the gale-force winds whistling down Broadway, the original Sophie Bell can't help herself. She holds up one hand and cries, "Stop!" Before she goes any further, she's just got to say thank you to:

The House of Razorbill: Publisher Ben Schrank, captain of the ship, floater of boats. Editor Rebecca "E is for I'm So Overwhelmed, Find Me One Month More Please, The Handshake Idea Was Genius, You're So Pretty and Smart, Did I Mention How Much You Look Like Iris?" Kilman. Designer Kristin Smith, who wouldn't be caught dead in *the horror* pleated-front khakis: Where would the UVs be without your art direction? Managing Editor Vivian Kirklin— sorry. Sorry again. Sorry for this one, even more sorry for the next one, and I may as well say a preemptive sorry now for the one after that. Marketing Director Erin Dempsey.

Publicist Marisa Russell. All the dedicated Penguin people I don't even know who are doing their utmost to propagate the purple.

Chris Battle, the creator of archetypes.

Ethen Beavers, the awesome executioner. Thanks for changing the clown—a phrase that from this point forward can be a euphemism for whatever you want.

The founding mothers: Jocelyn Davies, the first reader in my mind for at least the first half of the first draft; and Micol Ostow—oh, for those halcyon days of three pages.

The three graces: Aimee Friedman, my emergency cheerleader; Jazan Higgins, deliverer of shocking bolts of clarity, guardian of the chocolate drawers; and Marijka Kostiw, my fantasy personal stylist. If only I could write books as easily as epic, obsessive e-mails and text messages. . . .

Barry Cunningham, the sixth Beatle.

An old-school new-wave shout-out to the B-52's for their eponymous debut album and its follow-up, Wild Planet, which soundtracked me through Opal's party.

While this book was being written, downstairs they drilled through bricks. Outside, on rusted dinosaurs, they ripped up concrete, then covered the wound with fuming asphalt. And on a Monday in October, the ocean washed away the island's brief history. Special thanks to Kevin, who managed the damage while I apologized for deadlines.

For Cornelius, forever. Fiona, Eila, and Niamh, sparkle on. As for Siobhán McGowan? Some say she's from Mars. Or one of the seven stars. That shine after 3:30 in the morning.

Well, she isn't!

LOOK OUT FOR THE NEXT

VIOMAZING ADVENTURE FROM

THE **ULTRA VIOLETS**

WITH BOOK THREE:

LILAC ATTACK!

When **SOPHIE BELL** isn't busy scribbling the super-sparkly adventures of the Ultra Violets, she's refreshing her French, attempting to African dance, going solo to rock shows, and scouring thrift shops for other people's old clothes. All at the same time. She lives in Brooklyn, New York, with way too many books but still no sofa.

ETHEN BEAVERS grew up in Oregon and currently lives in California. He was about thirty years old when he entered the professional artist field (it's never too late to try). He works in comic books and children's publishing and is the regular artist for the *New York Times* bestselling series NERDS. He likes fly fishing for trout and root beer. And cartoons. He's married to a wonderful gal and is the second of seven children.